The Mermaid Queen

Published by SparkPress, a BookSparks imprint,
A division of SparkPoint Studio, LLC
Phoenix, Arizona, USA, 85007
www.gosparkpress.com

Published 2021
Printed in the United States of America
Print ISBN: 978-1-68463-113-1
E-ISBN: 978-1-68463-114-8

Library of Congress Control Number: 2021914647

Illustrations by Jonathan Stroh
Interior design by Tabitha Lahr

Witches of Orkney
Volume Four:

THE MERMAID QUEEN

ALANE ADAMS

spark press

To Charlee Day! Keep on flipping!

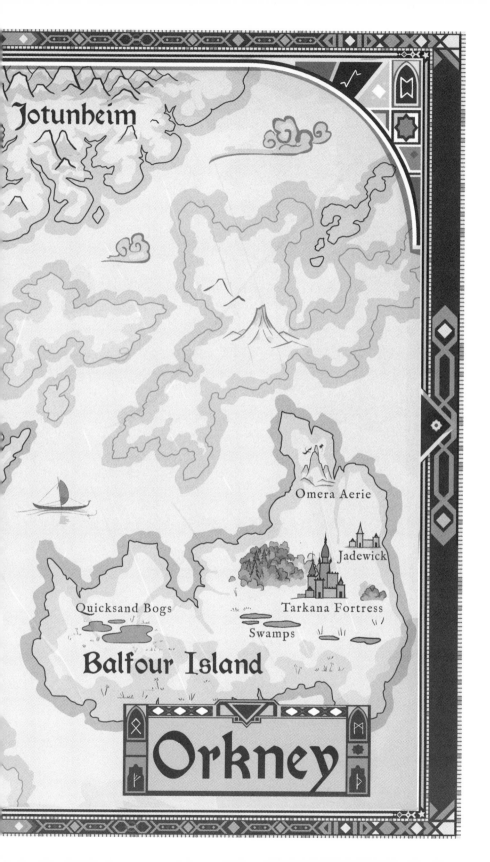

Jotunheim

Omera Aerie

Jadewick

Quicksand Bogs

Tarkana Fortress

Swamps

Balfour Island

Orkney

Prologue

Asgard

Ancient Days

The giant serpent thrashed against the chains binding him. Specially made by the dwarves of Gomara, the chains were sworn to be unbreakable, although Jormungand, the Midgard Serpent, did his best to prove that wrong. The other end of the chain was wrapped tightly around Odin's fist as he dragged the creature across the seas toward where the water was deepest.

Beneath Odin's feet was the mighty Skidbladnir, the ship of the gods. The ship could fly in the clouds as easily as it sailed on the waters.

At his side, the goddess Vor shook her head. "You know this will end badly."

Odin grunted. "Justice must be served."

"It is Loki who betrayed your trust, although even I do not believe he meant to harm Baldur."

Pain lanced Odin's heart all over again. His beloved son had been invincible—except for one weakness. Only the thorn of the simple mistletoe could fell him. Loki had known that. Used that. And now Baldur was lost to the shadows of the underworld, never to shine his light on the world again.

Anger roiled in Odin's heart. For all his charm, Loki was evil, and his children were no better. Fenrir, the ravenous wolf, had already been chained to a rock in the center of the ocean; Helva, the goddess of death, cast into the darkest underworld, never to see the light of day. The remaining offspring, Jormungand, would not be missed. The serpent had grown so large wrapped around Midgard that he had swallowed his own tail. If left unchecked, who knew what havoc he would wreak on the unprotected world of men? No. Ridding the world of Loki and his miserable children was just and right.

"It matters not whether he meant it, Vor, and you know it," Odin answered. "The price must be paid. Loki has been sent to live out his days in chains, and the world will be better off without his children roaming it."

Vor laid a hand on his arm. "It won't bring Baldur back."

"No. But one day I'll find a way. I haven't given up."

Vor's face lightened with understanding. "You have a plan."

"Not yet. I only know that when the time is right, I'll get him back myself if I have to."

He raised his hand, calling a halt. Behind him, a line of Valkyrie warriors, each holding another length of chain, paused midflight. Their golden armor glittered in the sunlight, wings fluttering as they waited.

Odin clasped his hands over his head and shouted, "Mighty Aegir, god of the seas, I command you to rise."

There was silence. Even Jormungand paused in his thrashing, and the sea grew eerily calm. And then a ripple crossed the water's surface. It turned into a whirlpool that foamed and tossed the ship about. Jormungand let out a screech, trying to snap at a Valkyrie, but the warrior nimbly somersaulted out of the way.

And then Aegir rose from the sea, riding a magnificent seahorse with purple-and-green scales, which he guided with a golden harness. His long, thin beard was pointed, and he carried a staff made of whale bone. On his head he wore a crown made of seashells.

"Odin. What brings you to my part of the world?" His eyes fell on the monstrous serpent, and anger blazed. "The Midgard Serpent doesn't belong in my seas."

"Aegir, friend, I had no choice. The serpent is a threat to mankind, and I swore vengeance on Loki for harming my son Baldur."

The sea god stared at the serpent, looking doubtful. "He will not be easy to contain. He is far too powerful."

"He will continue to shrink in size if he's contained. Surely you have a prison that can hold him."

Aegir hesitated.

"Or I can leave him to roam about your seas."

Aegir scowled. "There is a place," he said grudgingly. "Deep underwater."

"How will he eat?" Vor asked. "He mustn't be punished for what he is."

"He will find a fresh supply of fish to satisfy him." Aegir turned and waved his staff over the water. The whirlpool swirled wider and wider, growing ever deeper. "Come."

Odin guided Skidbladnir down the side of the whirlpool, dragging Jormungand behind him as they followed Aegir into the depths of the seas. Seawater surrounded them on all sides, held back by Aegir's powers.

At the bottom, they landed before a mountain of rock. Aegir held out his staff, and blue light blazed out and hit the mountain's surface. Slowly, the rock slid sideways to reveal a cavern that encircled a dark pool of water. Bars lined the far side, beyond which a small trail led up to a round opening.

"The feeding chute." Aegir pointed at the opening with his staff.

"This is too small," Vor said. "How will he move about?"

"The chasm of water is deep," Aegir said. "He will have ample opportunity to swim without being able to escape."

Odin nodded. "Are you sure it will hold him?"

"As sure as solid stone can hold any beast."

Odin signaled to the Valkyrie. Using their swords, they prodded the serpent forward into the large pool, then released the chains that bound him. The serpent sank from sight, his massive body slithering into the water until the tail disappeared.

Odin was about to turn away when Jormungand burst out of the water, striking at Odin's face.

With swift reflexes, he grabbed the snake's jaws, holding them apart. Jormungand's fangs glistened with a deadly venom that could fell even the most powerful of the gods. If not for the Belt of Strength Odin wore, the snake would have had his way.

"Not today, Jormungand." Odin heaved him backward against the opposite wall, and the serpent slithered back into the water.

As they turned to leave, Odin spied a small gate. "How does that open?"

"With this." Aegir held his hand out, revealing a silver key.

Odin smiled and palmed it. "It might come in handy. If I ever want him released."

"Why would you ever want the serpent released?"

"The future has a way of surprising us."

Chapter 1

Abigail stared sightlessly out the window of her attic room, toward the dark canopy of swamp trees outside the walls of the Tarkana Fortress. Inside she felt hollow, as if someone had carved her very soul out of her body. She had given everything she had to fix her mistakes, and it had only made things worse. Bitterness burned in her chest. She had trusted that mermaid Capricorn and been made a fool.

The mermaid queen had used the spellbook with Vertulious returned to it to open the prison of a dangerous creature: the Midgard Serpent—said to be able to wrap himself around the entire world and destroy it as well. Now, according to Vor, not just Orkney but the entire universe was in jeopardy, and it was all her fault.

There was a light rap on her door, quickly followed by a creak as it opened.

"You missed dinner." Calla's voice was hesitant.

"I'm not hungry." Food tasted like ashes in her mouth.

Calla's footsteps moved closer, but Abigail didn't pull her gaze from the swamps, as if they could give her the answers she sought.

"Cook made jookberry pie. I thought you—"

"I'm not hungry," Abigail cut in. "Did I not make that clear?"

Calla sighed. "Yes, Abigail. You did. But even a witchling has to eat. So tell me what's so wrong that you've turned into a recluse. Hugo's worried."

"Hugo needs to mind his own business."

Calla put a hand on her arm. "Since when do you care so little for your closest friends?"

Abigail shrugged her off. "Since when does the leader of the secondlings bother with a failed witch?" After excelling at all of her classes, Calla had been appointed Head Witchling of the secondlings and wore the gold *T* pin proudly on her shoulder.

"You're not a failed witch."

"I will be soon."

Abigail hadn't studied, had hardly attended classes since her meeting with Vor, claiming an unspecified illness. Surprisingly, Madame Hestera had instructed Madame Vex to leave her be. The coven leader was probably happy to get rid of her.

"It's not too late. I can help you get caught up."

Abigail laughed. "Why bother, when this place won't even be here soon?"

"What does that mean?"

Immediately regretting her words, Abigail turned to face Calla, who had a perplexed look on her face. "Thank you for bringing me dinner. You can leave now."

"No. I'm not leaving. This has gone far enough. Tell me what's going on."

"Or what?" A ball of witchfire appeared over Abigail's hand. "What are you going to do?"

Calla's own witchfire ignited. The once glitch-witch had caught up, and her powers were now second only to Abigail's. "I'm going to show you that you can't keep carrying whatever this is alone. That you have friends who want to help. Now, eat the pie before I singe your pigtails."

Abigail's stomach let out a gurgle, and she let the witchfire die out. "Fine. If it will get you to leave."

She scraped up a bite with the fork and savored the sweet taste of jookberries, then frowned as a bitter taste made her ask, "What kind of pie did you say this is?"

But Calla's face had grown longer, as if her chin were sagging to the floor, and her eyes were large. The room spun in a circle, and then Abigail fell into a spiraling hole.

Chapter 2

Outside Abigail's window, Hugo bobbed on the back of Big Mama, anxiously studying the courtyard below. It was dinnertime, and the witchlings were in the dining hall, but it paid to be observant. The stone of the dormitory tower radiated warmth from the day's sun. Beyond the fortress walls, he could make out the dark treetops of the swamp.

It had been weeks since he and Abigail had returned from Garamond, fresh off their victory of defeating Vertulious and averting a terrible war. Abigail should have been ecstatic, but instead she'd been refusing to see him. She hadn't even offered an excuse, just ignored his every message. In desperation, he had turned to Calla, and the two of them had plotted a way to get Abigail to open up about whatever was bothering her.

The shutters flew open, and Calla's worried face appeared.

"She's out."

"Can you lift her?"

"No, but I have a spell."

Calla disappeared back inside, and Abigail floated into sight and out the window. Hugo reached out to snag her ankle and tug her onto the back of Big Mama.

The Omera snorted, twisting her head to study Abigail, a rumbling snarl in her chest.

"It's okay, Big Mama. We're trying to help her," Hugo said.

The Omera chuffed but waited for Calla to climb on before taking flight.

They landed in the clearing in front of Baba Nana's hovel with a *thud*. Hugo slid down first, taking Abigail by the shoulders and easing her off. Calla jumped down and grabbed her ankles. They carried her into the small shack, then set her down gently on a pile of blankets they'd arranged by the fire. It was springtime, but there was still a nip in the air.

Hugo knelt by her side. "When is she going to wake up? You didn't give her too much, did you?"

"No, the potion is made from the kava kava fruit. It's powerful, but she'll wake up soon. What are we going to say when she does?"

"Whatever it takes to stop her from incinerating us with witchfire for kidnapping her," he said wryly.

Abigail groaned. One hand went to her head, then her eyes fluttered open. "Where am I?"

"Baba Nana's," Hugo said.

"How did I—the pie!" She turned angry eyes on Calla. "You tricked me."

"I did it for your own good," Calla said firmly. "And don't even think of using magic on us. We're your friends, and you won't tell us what's wrong. According to Hugo, everything is fixed. We have peace, and Vertulious is gone."

Abigail sat up, wrapping her arms around her knees. "He's not gone."

"Is that what's wrong? Is he bothering you again?" Calla asked.

"No. I haven't heard from him."

"Then what is it?" Hugo asked. "Please, tell us. You don't have to carry whatever it is alone."

"Yes, I do." Abigail angrily got to her feet. "You had no right to bring me here. I want to go home."

She marched to the door and tugged on it, but the door wouldn't budge. She whirled on Calla. "Let me out."

The girl folded her arms. "No."

A ball of witchfire sprang into Abigail's hand. "Let me out, or I'll burn this place down."

Hugo stepped forward. "Abigail, I know you won't hurt us. Whatever it is, you can trust us. Whatever you've done, I was probably right there with you."

She glared at him a moment longer, and then her shoulders sagged, and the witchfire winked out. She looked shattered, hollowed out from the inside.

"You don't understand," she whispered. "It's too terrible. I don't even know if it's true. I keep waiting, but nothing happens."

Calla led her to the fireplace and patted the sagging couch. "Sit. Spill it."

Abigail sat, looking grateful to be off shaky legs. Hugo sat on the other side of her and waited.

"When we returned from Garamond, I was so happy. I mean, we had finally solved everything, right?"

"Right," Hugo said. "Vertulious was banished, and the war was over."

"Only that's not what happened, not exactly," Abigail said. "Vor came to me."

"Vor, goddess of wisdom Vor?" Calla's eyes went wide.

Abigail nodded. "She's been a friend, sort of. Helping

me from time to time. She's the one who gave me the news. I was such a fool."

"Why?"

"I trusted the wrong person."

"Who?" Hugo asked.

Abigail spat the word out. "Capricorn."

Hugo frowned. "The queen of the mermaids betrayed you? But how?"

"She wanted the spellbook for one reason—to trick Vertulious into helping her release the Midgard Serpent."

Calla gasped, her hands flying to her lips. "We learned about him in Animals, Beasts, and Creatures class. He's a terrible monster. They say he can destroy the world with the force of his tail, turning it all to rubble."

Abigail nodded mutely. "And Capricorn has released him."

"But why would she do that?" Hugo asked.

"Vor didn't say. She only told me that if he wasn't put back into his prison, then it wasn't just Orkney that was threatened but the gods themselves."

There was shocked silence.

"You see? I didn't fix anything at all," she said bitterly. "I just made things worse, as worse as they can be."

"Hey." Hugo grabbed her hand. It was ice cold. "You did everything you could to stop the Orkadians and the witches from entering a pointless war."

Calla stood, pacing briskly back and forth. "I don't understand. My mother has spoken of Capricorn but never said anything about her being power hungry."

"Why does your mother choose to be a mermaid and not a witch?" Abigail asked.

Calla flushed. "She doesn't choose. It's just . . . it's complicated. She doesn't talk about it much, but I overheard my great-aunt Hestera talking. She said something about my grandfather being a merman. She can take both witch form and mermaid form."

"What about you?" Hugo asked. "Can you take a mermaid form?"

She shrugged. "I've never tried. I had a hard enough time getting my magic. I've never even been near the water."

"You don't swim?" Abigail asked.

Calla shook her head. "I didn't want . . . I mean, the slightest touch of saltwater and I could change into one of those creatures! My mother is used to it, but she wanted me to grow up as a witchling."

"You might have to try," Hugo said, "if we're going to confront Capricorn and get her to send Jormungand back to his prison."

"How are we going to do that?" Abigail asked. "Even if Calla were a mermaid, it's not like Capricorn would listen to her."

"We have to do something. If Jormungand really is loose in the seas around Orkney, someone has to stop him."

Abigail threw her hands up. "This is why I didn't tell you, because I knew you would want to do something foolish."

"Like running off to Jotunheim and getting Thor's hammer?" he asked quietly.

"Yes! And see how that turned out?" she shouted. "Perfectly awful."

"It's not your fault that Capricorn betrayed you. You tried to do the right thing."

"But it's not okay. Everyone—this world—could be lost because of my actions."

He put a hand on her arm. "So if we do nothing, what happens?"

She was silent for a moment. "Capricorn wins."

"And if we try to stop her?"

"She might still win, but—"

"But she might lose."

She raised her eyes to his. "What if something worse happens?"

"What could be worse than the end of the entire universe?"

Abigail laughed. "I don't know, but knowing us, we'll find it. Okay." Her face lightened. "I guess you're right. Doing nothing won't stop it from happening. We need someone who knows a lot about the mermaids. Calla, have you heard from your mother recently?"

She shook her head. "Not in weeks. Sometimes I don't hear from her for months. Baba Nana could help if only she were awake. She told me stories about the mermaids when I was young. Madame Vex has scoured the library searching for a way to reverse the spell on her."

Melistra had cast a chill spell on Baba Nana the night Vertulious returned that was slowly turning her body into a block of ice. Only the counter magic of Madame Vex kept death at bay, but even her magic wasn't powerful enough to counteract the spell. The old witch remained in a state of near death.

"Maybe if we worked together?" Abigail looked at Calla. "Our magic is potent when we combine it."

Calla frowned, thinking. "What if we got more witches to help?"

"More?"

"Yes. What if we got the coven to work together?"

"The witches will never stand for bringing Baba Nana back. They thought of her as a traitor."

Calla sagged. "You're right."

"But that doesn't mean we can't find some witchlings to help."

Chapter 3

Abigail stepped into her Magical Maths class. Truthfully, it felt good to be back. She'd been in a fog for weeks. Hugo was right—taking action was better than waiting for the world to end.

She looked around the room. Endera sat up front, flanked by Glorian and Nelly. The ever-popular Portia chatted with a circle of witchlings. Calla had intercepted Madame Vex to give Abigail some time to speak directly to the class.

Clutching her book bag to her chest, she strode to the front of the room. The witchlings all stopped chattering and watched her, curious.

"Um, hi," she said.

"Look who's back." Endera sneered. "We thought you'd packed up and left. We even had a farewell party."

The other girls sniggered.

"I'm still here. Back in Garamond, we worked together, Endera. We stopped Vertulious."

"What's your point?" Endera snapped. "You would have let the coven fail if I hadn't stepped in."

Abigail bit her tongue. She needed the girl on her side. "Right. I mean, we couldn't have done it without you."

The witchling preened.

"There is another witch that needs our help," Abigail went on.

Endera stiffened, her face losing color. "Do not speak that name."

"Baba Nana lies in a state of near death. We can—"

"I said don't speak that name!" Endera stood and slapped her hands on the desk. "Or so help me, I will—"

The door opened and Madame Vex stepped in, staring down her long, thin nose at Abigail in surprise. Calla crowded in behind her.

"Abigail, did I give you permission to teach my class?"

"No, Madame Vex."

"Then please explain what you are doing."

"I wanted to ask the secondlings if they would help me bring back Baba Nana."

Madame Vex frowned. "I have been tending to her for months and tried every spell I know to bring her back. Do you really think some secondlings have a better chance than a witch as powerful as me?"

When Abigail remained silent, she raised an eyebrow. "This from a witchling close to flunking out of the Tarkana Academy?"

Endera snorted with laughter, earning a glare from Madame Vex.

"I'm going to make up the work I missed," Abigail said.

"Final exams are in two weeks. I suggest you don't delay. Take your seat, we have many things to cover today."

By the time class ended, Abigail's head was spinning. Madame Vex had spent the entire class time writing out the formulas needed to make beetlewing potions in different potencies and batch sizes. She was hopelessly lost. As she was dragging herself from class, Madame Vex called out to her. The teacher waited until the other girls left before putting a gentle hand on Abigail's shoulder.

"I appreciate your efforts to bringing Baba Nana back, but I'm afraid it's too late. The old witch is nearly gone. You should be spending your time on catching up."

"I will. Starting tomorrow. Please, do you have any ideas?"

She pursed her lips. "I've tried every spell I can think of to reverse the chill spell Melistra cast but so far I've failed."

Abigail had a sudden thought. "What if Baba Nana was wrong?"

"What do you mean?"

"When Calla and I found her, she told us Melistra had cast a chill spell, but what if she was wrong?"

Madame Vex's eyes narrowed. "I wonder . . . there are some potions that can have a similar effect, but this one would have to be immensely powerful. Melistra wasn't known for her potions."

"What about Madame Radisha?" Their Positively Potent Potions teacher was an expert on making potions but Madame Vex shook her head.

"Melistra and Madame Radisha did not see eye to eye. She would have never given her such a powerful potion. I suggest you speak with Madame Camomile. She may have an idea."

Madame Camomile was their Fatal Flora teacher and knew every noxious plant in the realm.

Abigail curtsied. "Thank you, Madame Vex. I will speak to her today."

She hurried into the hall where Calla was waiting, excited to tell her about the new plan, when a hand latched on to her shoulder, whirling her around.

"That witch should have died. She betrayed my mother." Two angry spots of color stained Endera's cheeks. Glorian and Nelly hovered behind her.

Abigail shrugged free. "You're wrong. Melistra went after Baba Nana because Baba Nana wanted to stop your mother from bringing Vertulious back."

Endera stabbed a finger against Abigail's chest. "My mother wanted to bring back *Rubicus*, the greatest he-witch to ever live. She was betrayed. Maybe Baba Nana was working with that alchemist."

"Is that really what you believe?"

Endera's lip quivered slightly, then firmed. "Doesn't matter. That old hag's not coming back. And no one here is going to help you." She pushed past Abigail, flouncing down the hall. Glorian and Nelly gave Abigail a helpless shrug and then slunk after Endera.

Abigail sighed. "Do you think she's ever going to get over her need for revenge?"

Calla hooked her arm in Abigail's. "Doubt it. She's a witch. We don't forget. Or forgive."

Chapter 4

Hugo hurried up the steps of the Balfin School for Boys. Now that the threat of war was over, things had gotten a lot better at school. Oskar no longer bullied him, and participation in the Balfin Boys' Brigade—along with those stiff military uniforms—wasn't required.

He took his trusted notebook out of his pocket and thumbed to a clean page. If there was one thing Hugo liked, it was a problem to puzzle out, and this one was big, even bigger than stopping a war. He wrote down *Mermaids* and then tapped the page. What did he know about them?

Their queen was Capricorn, and she lived in an underwater city named Zequaria. He and Abigail had visited when they'd been hauled overboard by one of her minions. The mermaid queen had seemed cold, but Hugo never imagined she would plot to use the spellbook to release the Midgard Serpent.

He headed straight for his favorite history professor's classroom. It was still early, but Oakes was usually in.

"Come in," the professor called at Hugo's knock.

Hugo opened the door, and Oakes greeted him with a smile. "Hugo, my boy, what can I do for you?"

Oakes had been reinstated to his teaching position after the war had ended, and he seemed to credit Hugo.

"Well, sir, I was hoping you could tell me about mermaids."

"One caught your eye then?" he asked with a wink. "I hear they're quite beautiful."

"Yes. I mean no, no one's caught my eye, but they are quite beautiful."

"Then you've met one?" Oakes sat down at a desk and motioned for Hugo to sit across from him. "Perhaps it is I who should be asking you about them."

"They live in a domed city under the sea. Their queen is Capricorn. Are you familiar with her?"

"Only vaguely," he said with a wave of his hand. "It seems like she had a feud with the king of the sea, Aegir himself." He waggled his eyebrows. "She had a thing for him, and he spurned her for a mermaid named Ran. She never forgave him."

Hugo wrote that down in his notebook. "What about the Midgard Serpent?"

Oakes's brows went up. "The serpent who could encircle the world and swallow his own tail? We don't exactly study that in history. Seems to fall under beasts and such."

"Yes, of course. I just wondered."

"If I knew any good stories?"

"Yes."

"Hmm, I remember back when I was a student, I had a professor who was fascinated by the story of how Jormungand came to be trapped in an underwater cell. You've heard of the mischief maker Loki?"

"Of course, everyone's heard the stories."

"Well, did you know Jormungand is his son?"

"No. That seems . . . odd. Isn't Jormungand a serpent?"

"Yes, there's no accounting for the offspring of the gods. His other child is an oversized wolf named Fenrir, and his third, Helva, is the goddess of death."

Hugo wrote all that down in his notebook. "That's an interesting family—but that doesn't explain how Jormungand ended up in a prison under the water."

"Loki did something unforgivable. Odin and his wife Frigga had a son named Baldur, and he was their favorite. They made sure Baldur was invincible. Loki was determined to find a weakness just to poke fun at Odin, who was so proud of his son, so he disguised himself and visited Frigga in her chambers and found out Baldur had one weakness."

"What was it?"

"The thorn of the mistletoe."

"Really? Loki attacked him with a mistletoe branch?"

"Not Loki. He got Baldur's blind brother, Hod, to do it for him. The poor lad didn't know what he was doing, and Baldur took it in good fun. Until he fell down and didn't get up. When it came out Loki was behind it, Odin was furious."

"What did he do?"

"He wanted to end Loki right there and then, but Frigga demanded that Loki suffer for eternity. So Odin sent him to a cave deep underground where water drips on him daily. Then he banished Loki's children."

"But if Jormungand is so big, how did Odin capture him?"

"He had a special set of chains made by the dwarves of Gomara, strong enough to withstand the strength of the serpent, and then he and his Valkyrie warriors dragged Jormungand across the sea. With his powers contained, the serpent's body shrank to a more reasonable size—still massive but not world-ending. When Odin reached the deepest part, he called on the sea god Aegir to place him in an underground lair."

"So he's been there ever since."

"You wouldn't want him to get out."

"Because?"

"Because he's not going to be happy to have been locked up for centuries. I imagine he'd want revenge. Wouldn't you?"

Hugo nodded.

Oakes stood. "But fortunately there's no chance of that happening, now is there?"

Chapter 5

Abigail and Calla hurried to their Fatal Flora class, eager to speak with their teacher about Abigail's theory that Baba Nana's curse had been caused by a powerful potion and not a spell.

Madame Camomile entered from the greenhouse attached to their classroom carrying a pot in her hands. The teacher was tall and thin like a sapling, with long arms that waved in the air whenever she discussed her latest poisonous potion. Her hair was always full of leaves and twigs, as though she'd just been rolling around in a bush. Once, when one of the secondlings had tried to tug a leaf out of the tangles, she'd let out a yelp and slapped the girl's hand, as if the leaf were *growing* out of her head. She carefully set the potted plant down on a table.

"My dear secondlings, this is a rare opportunity for you indeed. Come closer, please."

The secondlings scraped their chairs back and hurried forward. Abigail elbowed her way up front, staring down at the odd plant. It had a sturdy green stalk with spiky leaves, and a large green and purple bud with its petals folded closed. It smelled faintly like spoiled meat.

"This is a very rare plant I've only read about in books," the teacher said excitedly. "I found it on the eastern shores of the swamps when I got lost on my way back from my usual gathering of herbs."

Endera stuck a finger out to poke at the bud, but Madame Camomile slapped her hand away just as the flower unfurled. A forked leaf resembling a serpent's tongue shot out of the petals, striking at the spot where Endera's finger had been. Thick thorns made sharp fangs along the flower's inner lining, mimicking a serpent's jaw. It had no eyes, but it swayed in the air, searching for movement, before the forked leaf retreated back into the petals.

"What was that?" Endera asked shakily.

"That is *Venemous lilium*, otherwise known as the cobra lily. Its venom leaves the victim in excruciating pain until the point of death. It's said it can even sicken the gods."

"Is there a cure?" Portia asked, her eyes large in her face.

"Why would a witch want a cure?" Madame Camomile trilled. "One doesn't extract its venom unless one wants their victim to suffer. Now, I will instruct you on the safe extraction of the poison." She pulled on a thick pair of leather gloves and picked up a hollow metal tube with a sharpened end. "Careful, girls, it isn't going to like this."

The witchlings took a step back, gasping as Madame Camomile jabbed the furled bud with the tube. Its mouth snapped at the air, searching for something to attack.

"Can it see us?" Glorian asked, stepping closer and waving her hand. The forked tongue struck at her fingers, and she quickly snatched her hand back.

"No, Glorian, it's a plant. It doesn't have eyes. It can sense air movement and the warmth of your skin. There, that's got it." She drew the metal tube out and carried it to a small workbench.

She released her finger off the top of the tube and let the venom trickle into a ceramic bowl. It was a small amount, less than a teaspoon, and a pale yellow color like tree sap.

"What are you going to do with it?" Endera asked.

"I've had a special request for a—" Madame Camomile abruptly stopped, and her face turned slightly green. "That is, the High Witch Council is always curious about any new discoveries." She clapped her hands swiftly. "Back to your desks now and open up your textbook to the section on harvesting poisonous mushroom caps."

Abigail and Calla exchanged glances. Their flora teacher had let something slip she hadn't intended. Someone wanted a strong poison—but who did they want to poison?

While Madame Camomile droned on about the proper drying technique of mushroom caps, Abigail whispered to Calla.

"Did you notice her reaction? When she mentioned the poison?"

Calla nodded, keeping her head down as she pretended to take notes. "Who do you suppose requested it?"

"I don't know, but it sounded like she was talking about someone on the High Witch Council."

Madame Camomile cast them a withering glare and they fell silent.

The two witchlings approached the teacher after class. Madame Camomile was busy snipping some of the plants she kept on a shelf near the window.

"Excuse me, Madame Camomile," Abigail began. "We were wondering if we could ask a question."

She continued her clipping. "I must say I was surprised to see you back in class, Abigail. I thought you had given up."

"I'm sorry. I'm planning on making up the work I've missed if you'll let me."

She sniffed. "I heard about what you did, traveling to Jotunheim and facing down a giant. A lot for a secondling to handle. I suppose if you turn in all your missed work by final exams, I can allow it."

"I'll help her," Calla said quickly.

Relief flooded Abigail. It would be hard, but she would do every assignment needed to keep her place at the Tarkana Witch Academy. "May I ask another favor?"

"You want me to help you find a cure for Baba Nana?"

Abigail blinked. "Yes! But how did you know?"

"Madame Vex mentioned something in passing this morning. I didn't know the old witch all that well, and unlike others in the coven, I have no hard feelings toward her. I do, however, owe Madame Vex a favor."

"Do you know of any plants that Melistra might have used to make a potion?" Calla asked.

Madame Camomile's brows went up. "You think she used a potion on her?"

Abigail shrugged. "It would explain why no one, not even Madame Vex, can reverse the spell."

"Because it's not a spell at all," Madame Camomile mused. "Interesting theory. There aren't many witches capable of making a potion like that. I suppose we could try giving her some broth made from *Metopium toxifera*. It's a sort of universal cure-all against most potions. It may neutralize it enough to bring her around."

"Do you have some on hand?" Abigail asked.

"No, I'm afraid I haven't used it in some time. You can find a drawing of it in your textbook. It grows about waist high and has purplish leaves and small yellow berries. The bush grows out in the swamps in a sunny spot. You just have to find a bush, harvest some berries, crush them into a paste, and make a tea with it. Of course, you can't use too many berries, or it will have the opposite effect. And you have to make sure they're ripe, or it won't do anything but turn your stomach. Be sure to give her half a cup, not an ounce more, or the cure will finish the job."

"That's it?" Abigail asked. "Just find the right bush, pick the perfect berries, and make a tea with just the right amount?"

The teacher smiled, and the leaves in her hair rustled. "Easy enough for a secondling as clever as yourself. Bring the berries to me if you find some, and I'll help make up the potion. Now run along, I must feed my beautiful *Venemous lilium* before it wilts with hunger." She pulled a small mouse out of her pocket, dangling it over the plant by its tail as they hurried away.

Chapter 6

Abigail counted the minutes until it was time to meet Hugo after school. Now that she'd decided to act instead of sitting around waiting for the world to end, she was anxious to get started. She'd asked Calla to join them, and the girl was waiting under the jookberry tree, intently reading from her Hexes book.

"There you are." Calla set down her textbook and patted the spot next to her.

Abigail sat, putting her face in her hands. "I can't believe how behind I am. Look how far you are in your Hexes book. I'm not even halfway."

"You'll catch up," Calla said. "I promise I'll help all I can."

Abigail sighed. "It would take a miracle."

"I can help too." Hugo dropped down from the branches overhead, landing spryly on his feet. "I'm really good at Magical Maths."

"Thanks Hugo, I'll need all the help I can get with exams coming up soon. That is, if Jormungand hasn't ended the world by then. What did you find out?"

"I spoke with one of my professors. The good news is Jormungand's powers have been contained for centuries—it will take him a while to get back to his full size and power."

"What else?"

"It seems like Capricorn had a crush on Aegir."

"The sea god?" Abigail asked.

"Yes, and he rejected her."

"So she's going to have the serpent destroy the world because she was jilted?" Calla said, aghast. "That's awful."

"Capricorn said she was the queen of all sea creatures, remember?" Abigail asked. "So what more does she want?"

Hugo tapped his notebook. "Maybe it's not enough. Maybe she wants what Aegir has—the power to rule over the sea itself."

Abigail sighed. "I guess it doesn't matter why she's doing it. We need to find a way to capture Jormungand before he grows big enough to destroy this place."

"Baba Nana could help," Calla said. "She taught Advanced Beasts. Maybe she can tell us how to capture him. We need that cure."

"You found a cure?" Hugo asked.

"Maybe." Calla described the bush Madame Camomile had told them about. "It's somewhere out in the swamps."

"Er, the swamps?" Hugo looked nervous.

"Relax, Hugo, the viken is long gone," Abigail said. "I say we go now. There's still time before supper." She sprang to her feet and headed for the gate.

"It's not the viken I'm worried about. It's the sneevils and quicksand bogs," Hugo said as he scrambled to his feet. "What if we run into a wraith?"

Calla laughed. "A wraith? Really, Hugo, your imagination . . ."

"It's not my imagination. Professor Oakes believes that wraiths are real. He says they were a race of beautiful women who bragged about their beauty to Freya, the goddess of beauty, claiming they were ten times more beautiful than she was."

"And?"

He rolled his eyes. "Don't they teach you anything at the Tarkana Academy?"

She huffed. "We learn lots of things, right Calla?"

"Important things like spells and hexes," Calla agreed.

"Well, history is important too. Freya got so mad she stripped them of their souls and left them in limbo. They haunt places like this swamp."

"What's your point?" Abigail asked.

"It's just . . . jeez, aren't you ever afraid?"

Her brows drew together. "Of making mistakes that end the world? Daily. But of things in the swamp? No. I've got magic and so does Calla, and you've got brains enough for all of us. We'll be fine."

The gate swung shut behind them, and they stared at the dark, gnarled trees of the swamp.

"So which way?" Hugo asked.

"Madame Camomile said it needs a sunny spot with lots of boggy sand," Abigail said.

Hugo pondered it. "We could try heading east toward the old fortress. It gets the most sunlight on the island."

"Then lead on."

Endera watched the three figures disappear into the swamps.

"What now?" Nelly asked, slapping at a bug that landed on her cheek.

"Now we follow them," Endera said.

"But—" Glorian's face fell. "Cook said she would teach me how to make black cabbage pie."

"Stuff cabbage pie," Endera snapped. "We need to find out what Abigail is up to. You know she's always plotting to bring down this coven."

"She helped save the coven from Vertulious," Nelly pointed out.

Endera whirled, stabbing her finger against the girl's chest. "I'm the one who saved the coven. Without my powers, we would have never defeated Vertulious that day."

Nelly pushed her hand away. "We were there too, Endera. It wasn't just you."

"But she's the one who brought him back in the first place," Endera argued. "She was probably working with him all along."

"But I thought you said it was Baba Nana." Glorian said, flinching back when Endera whirled on her, shoving her face close to the other girl's.

"All of them are traitors!" she shouted. "And you will be too if you don't help me rid the coven of Abigail once and for all."

Turning away, Endera stomped off into the swamps, blindly heading in the direction of Abigail and the others. Tears blurred her eyes even as anger burned in her chest. It wasn't fair that everyone considered Abigail a hero. If it hadn't been for Abigail's interference, her mother would have brought Rubicus back as she'd planned, and everything would be just fine. But instead, her mother had died, and Vertulious had come back and ruined things even more.

She stopped, her chest heaving from exertion. The swamps were hot and muggy, and she undid the button at her collar, trying to catch her breath. Glorian and Nelly slunk up behind her.

"Sorry, Endera," Glorian said between breaths. "We didn't mean to upset you."

"I'm not upset." She kept her back to them as she scrubbed the tears away with her palms. "Now keep your mouths quiet. We don't want them to know we're following them."

Chapter 7

After a solid hour of walking, Hugo was beginning to think it had been a bad idea to rush off into the swamps without packing a flask of water or a packet of biscuits. Abigail marched on steadily, while he and Calla hurried after her. Sweat made Hugo's shirt cling to his back. Calla kept fanning herself, waving away the buzzing insects that hovered around them.

Abigail stopped suddenly, her head tilting to the side as if she were listening.

"I feel it too," Calla said softly.

Hugo looked around warily. "Feel what? Is it sneevils?"

"No," Calla said. "But something's watching us."

"Or someone," Abigail added.

Calla glanced around. "What do you want to do?"

"Maybe we should split up."

"Split up?" Hugo gulped. "I don't want to be alone out here."

"Don't be such a baby," Abigail said. "Nothing bad is going to happen."

"How do you know that?"

"I don't. Just . . . wait here. Calla and I will go ahead and circle back."

Hugo rocked back on his heels as the other two walked off. Nothing good had ever happened while venturing into the swamps. The first time, he'd been surrounded by sneevils—he could still see their horrible tusks as they'd snorted and pawed the ground, ready to charge. His neck prickled. He turned, studying the dark, twisted woods.

A twig snapped loudly.

"Hello?" His heart jumped in his chest. "Abigail?"

Sweat rolled down his back. There seemed to be eyes everywhere, watching him. Was that a shadow? Or a bush?

"Boo."

Hugo stifled a scream as a hand landed on his shoulder. He spun around, surprised to see Endera standing with her two cronies. Her face was red with exertion, and an ugly scratch marred her cheek.

"Endera. What are you doing out here?"

"Wondering the same thing. Why are you here? What are you planning?"

"Planning? Nothing. We're just looking for a plant. Something that can help Baba Nana."

Endera's face darkened with anger, but before the girl could shout at him, there was a loud rustle in the bushes nearby.

"Endera, what was that?" Glorian asked, her eyes round as she stared into the bushes.

"Zip it, Glorian. This Balfin boy is going to tell me what Abigail is really up to. Why did she stop going to classes?"

"That's none of your business," Hugo huffed.

"Endera, really, you should listen." Nelly joined Glorian to peer out into the swamps. "There's something moving around out there."

She glared at them. "Stuff it, both of you. It's just Abigail and Calla. They're probably lost." She turned back to Hugo. "So there *was* a reason she skipped classes. Madame Vex said she wasn't feeling well, but that wasn't it, was it?"

Hugo gritted his teeth. "It's up to Abigail to tell you."

The witchling stuck her finger under Hugo's chin, and her fingernail magically extended until it poked painfully into his skin. "Tell me before I make you bleed."

Hugo clenched his fists. "I'm not afraid of you."

"No?" Her eyes glowed with malice. "Who's going to miss a weak Balfin boy who got lost in the swamps?" The fingernail extended further, cutting into his skin, and then Nelly and Glorian screamed.

Hugo turned to find a tall figure cloaked in darkness staggering toward them, moaning loudly and waving its arms.

Abigail tromped through the swamps, carefully listening. She had a feeling it was Endera following them—the girl could never let anything go. Kneeling down, she ran her fingers over a set of boot prints. The wider boot was probably Glorian; the skinny heel, Nelly; and the solid step, Endera.

The bushes parted, and Calla's face appeared. "What did you find?"

"Just three nosy witchlings."

A mischievous look came over Calla's face. "Want to teach them a lesson?"

"What did you have in mind?"

Calla quickly explained her idea.

"Are you sure you can hold me?"

"I'm sure. Here, get on."

Abigail stepped up on a rock and carefully climbed onto her friend's shoulders.

Calla swayed, then steadied. "Now throw my cloak over your head, and let yours drape down, covering my face." She muttered a few soft words, and a black cloud swirled around them.

"That's amazing," Abigail said.

"If you went to Spells class, you'd know it too," Calla said, her voice muffled by the cloak.

Abigail stifled a giggle as they got closer to the clearing where she could see Endera grilling poor Hugo.

"Two steps to the right," she whispered.

She let out a groan and shook the branches of a gnarled tree as they stepped into the clearing. Waving her arms, she moaned louder. "Oooooooo."

The look on Endera's face was priceless. The girl looked scared out of her wits. She fumbled for witchfire, but she must have been too frightened to call it up, because it fizzled out in her hands. She grabbed Glorian and Nelly, hiding behind them as Hugo backpedaled across the clearing.

"Run!" Endera screamed. She turned and fled, followed closely by her two cronies.

Abigail threw off the cloak as Calla lowered her to the ground. The cloud around them vanished.

"That was amazing!" she said. "Did you see the look on Endera's face?"

"Like she'd seen a ghost," Calla said. They burst into a fit of laughter, collapsing against each other until Abigail remembered Hugo.

Wiping the tears from her eyes, she went and found Hugo. He was still hiding in the bushes. "Hugo, come out. I'm sorry. We just wanted to give them a scare."

Hugo climbed out from the bush, brushing off twigs, and pasted on a rueful grin. "Got me too. Nice trick." And then his eyes widened, and he took a step back.

"What's wrong?" Abigail looked over her shoulder but couldn't see anything, although the temperature seemed to drop a few degrees.

"I thought I saw something."

"Hugo, nice try," Calla said. "We're not going to fall for it."

"No, I'm serious. I think there's something there. Look."

A shadow flew past. This time Abigail saw it.

"Er, it's probably Endera getting back at us."

"That's not Endera," Calla said, shivering.

The temperature had dropped so much it felt as if they were in the chilly ice realm of Jotunheim and not the hot, muggy swamps on Balfour Island.

"What should we do?" Abigail asked. A fog swirled around their ankles, quickly rising to enclose them.

"I can't see," Calla waved her hand. "Can you?"

"No." Abigail called up a ball of witchfire, but the damp fog squelched it out.

"Quiet," Hugo said. "Listen."

The fog muted the swamp sounds, leaving them unable to see or hear clearly.

Something flew past Abigail's head, trailing icy fingers along her cheek.

"What was that?" she cried.

"I don't know," Calla said.

"I think they're wraiths," Hugo said. "Don't look at them and they can't hurt you."

Abigail closed her eyes as another brushed past her face. High-pitched screeching filled the clearing as more and more of the wispy creatures surrounded them.

Dark witch, come join us. You know you want to.

Abigail ignored the voice, keeping her eyes pressed shut. She could feel ghostly fingers trace her cheek, as though one was right in front of her. Others swirled overhead, their voices joining, calling to her.

Dark witch, we welcome you. You are one of us. See for yourself.

Abigail's eyelids fluttered. The need to look was overwhelming. Risking a peek, she looked into the face of a woman floating before her.

"She's beautiful," Abigail whispered. The wraith was young, with large eyes, high cheekbones, and a calm smile. And then the flesh rippled away, and the woman turned skeletal before her eyes.

"Abigail, don't look!" Hugo knocked her to the ground as the now-empty eye socket shot out a bolt of ice, but he wasn't in time to stop the shard from impaling her shoulder.

She gasped in pain.

"Abigail, are you all right?" Calla asked.

"It got me in the shoulder. Everyone, cover your eyes. Get back-to-back."

They huddled together, keeping their hands pressed against their eyes as the wraiths swirled around their heads. Suddenly the shard of ice was wrenched from Abigail's shoulder, and the sound of screeching faded. She risked another look. The fog was lifting.

"I think they're gone."

Hugo was studying her. "What happened to the ice shard?"

Abigail looked down. Her dress was torn where the shard had pierced her skin, and blood trickled out. "One of the wraiths took it." She gingerly touched the wound, hissing in pain.

"Here, let me see if I can help," Calla said. She placed her hand over the spot, murmuring a healing spell.

After a moment, the stinging pain receded, leaving a dull ache.

Calla patted Abigail's arm. "You'll be sore for a couple days. If it doesn't get infected, it should heal fine. Where do you think they came from?"

"Professor Oakes said they're drawn to powerful magic," Hugo said, then turned to Abigail. "Why did you open your eyes?"

"I couldn't help it," Abigail said. "They kept calling to me. You must have heard them."

The other two were silent.

A chill ran through her. *Had the wraiths only spoken to her?*

"Just all the screeching," Calla said. "What did they say?"

"I . . . I don't remember," she lied. "Look, if we're going to find that plant before it gets dark, we need to move. I don't want to spend the night out here."

Hugo helped her to her feet.

"Are you sure you feel up to it?" he asked.

She nodded, forcing a smile. "Calla's healing spell is working fine." But inside, she was shaking. The wraiths had singled her out, said she was one of them. What did that mean? They were dark creatures, beautiful on the outside but cold evil on the inside.

And what if they were right?

Chapter 8

It was Calla who found it. Not long after they'd fended off the wraiths, she spied a small bush with purplish leaves and small yellow berries Madame Camomile had described. They picked all the berries they could find, but it was late in the season and there weren't many left.

"Do you think it's enough?" Abigail asked as she eyed the half-full pouch.

"It has to be," Calla said. "There aren't any more, and we don't have time to go looking for another bush."

They hurried back through the swamps as twilight settled in, keeping an eye out for wraiths. The swamps were quickly becoming Abigail's least favorite place on Balfour Island. They nearly stumbled onto a mother sneevil with her little nurslings, but they managed to carefully back away before the tusked beast spied them and skewered them.

Relief filled her when they finally reached the gate to the gardens.

"That was quite an adventure," Hugo said with his usual cheerfulness.

"Let's take the berries to Madame Camomile right now," Calla said.

Abigail's shoulder was throbbing and she was exhausted from all their running around the swamps. "Madame Camomile will have retired to her chambers. Let's wait until the morning."

Calla looked disappointed, but she nodded. "I suppose one more day won't hurt."

They waved goodbye to Hugo and were heading down the path toward the fortress when a voice stopped them.

"Well, well, well. Just the witchling I was looking for."

Capricorn, the traitorous mermaid queen stepped out of the shadows.

"You." Witchfire sprang to Abigail's hands, the pain in her shoulder forgotten. "What are you doing here?"

"Who is this?" Calla asked.

The mermaid queen looked down at Calla haughtily. "Girl, don't you recognize your own queen?"

Capricorn's emerald colored hair was loosely piled atop her head, leaving two long curling strands along either side of her face. She wore a shimmering gown made from woven fish scales. She tilted her head to study Calla with calculating eyes. "You must be Calypha's brat. You should come for a swim sometime. I can show you the marvelous ways of being a mermaid."

"Calla is a witch," Abigail said.

"She is as much a mermaid as she is a witch," Capricorn snapped, flicking her hand out. A wave of power extinguished the witchfire in Abigail's hands. "But I'm not here to argue. I wanted to thank you for helping me."

Outrage fueled Abigail's outburst. "I didn't help you, you tricked me!"

Capricorn shrugged. "All the same, I owe you a debt, and I always pay my debts."

"You want to pay me back? Put the Midgard Serpent back in his cell," Abigail said.

Capricorn's eyes flared with anger. "Jormungand is none of your business, and I suggest you keep that information to yourself."

"Or what?"

The queen leaned in. "Or maybe my pet will encircle your puny island and swallow it whole."

"You wouldn't dare."

Capricorn smirked. "Try me." She straightened. "I'm just here to repay a favor, not argue about my future plans. Here." She pulled a familiar book from the folds of her gown and deposited it in Abigail's hands. "Consider us even."

Abigail recoiled at the sight of the hated spellbook. "I don't want it." She tried to pass the spellbook back to the mermaid queen, but the woman folded her arms.

"Too bad. It's yours, and I've returned it. We're even." Waggling her fingers goodbye, she sauntered through the gate, letting it slam closed behind her.

Abigail had half a mind to fling the hateful book into the deepest bog hole in the swamp, but it was too dangerous for just anyone to find. She shoved it into her book bag without looking at it.

"You really think she came here just to give you back the spellbook?" Calla asked.

"No. She's up to something. She must have been meeting someone."

"Hestera?"

"Maybe. Hestera wants revenge for our loss to the Orkadians. And Capricorn probably knows that. If we don't put that sea snake back in his cage, we might be right back where we started—in the middle of a disaster."

Back in her room, Abigail took out the wretched spellbook and set it carefully on the bed. She had thought she'd seen the last of it, but oddly, it didn't bother her the way it had before. Maybe because she had defeated Vertulious so thoroughly, he didn't scare her anymore.

"I know you're in there," she said. "So don't pretend like you're not. Come out. I want to see you."

The spellbook just sat there, as if it were nothing more than a book, but when Abigail waved her hand over the cover, she could feel the pulsing of magic.

"Fine. How about I toss the spellbook into a sneevil's den? They can chew the paper to pieces and line their nest with it."

The cover vibrated, and the book began to shake on the bed. Abigail waited, and then the cover flew open. A wisp of fog spiraled up and took shape and then Vertulious floated before her.

"What do you want?" He yawned widely, as if she'd woken him from a nap.

Abigail lashed into him. "Why would you do it? I know you have no heart but surely you realize releasing that serpent was the worst thing you could do."

He had the decency to look ashamed. "She promised to set me free, but she broke her word."

"Hmm, sounds like someone I know."

He scowled. "If you summoned me just to taunt me, I have better things to do."

"Such as torment another witchling?"

His face fell. "No. Sadly, I can't do much anymore."

Abigail's eyes narrowed. "What do you mean?"

He held his hands out. "I can't command the spellbook like I once did. It has a new master now."

Abigail frowned. "What does that mean?"

His eyes grew crafty. "Set me free and I'll tell you."

"I'm not going to release you. And besides, there's no source of power to bring you back. Odin's Stone was destroyed, remember?"

"I don't mean bring me back. I mean let me go." He waved a wispy hand in the air. "Help me pass on to another place."

Her heart stilled. "How would I do that?"

"Destroy the spellbook."

Abigail thought over his words. She was tempted to agree. She had made a promise to herself after destroying Odin's Stone that she would never use dark magic again. Her mother's words of warning were always in her head: *It is like a hunger that cannot be appeased. If you don't keep it at bay, it will devour you.* But the spellbook contained powerful spells. Spells she might need to defeat Capricorn.

"Sorry, I might need what's inside it."

He sighed. "And here I was thinking you were a witch with a heart."

"If you want to be released, help me defeat Capricorn. I need to send that serpent back to his lair before he destroys everything."

"If I help you, do I have your word you'll destroy the spellbook?"

Abigail sidestepped the question. "First things first. I need a healing spell to help Baba Nana." In case the potion didn't work.

"You have my healing spell. You used it once before."

"It's not strong enough."

His eyes gleamed. "There is a new spell you might try."

"New? What do you mean?"

He shrugged. "I told you the spellbook has a new master. But you won't like it."

"Why not?"

"You don't like the . . . darker spells."

She clenched her jaw against the memories of using his powerful and twisted magic. "If it's for a good reason, I'll do it."

He smiled wickedly. "That's my dark witch."

"Don't call me that."

She slammed the book shut, and the alchemist dissipated into wisps of air, but she could still hear his laughter echoing in her head.

Chapter 9

The next day as Abigail was heading to class, she caught the excited whispers of other witchlings in the hall talking about the monster loose in the swamps.

Calla caught up to her. "Have you heard?"

"Yes. Apparently, there's a monster on the loose."

A smile twitched Abigail's lips as she came up behind Endera, who was regaling a group of wide-eyed firstlings with the tale. Safina was among them, listening intently.

"We were out for a stroll, me and Glorian and Nelly, when suddenly we heard . . ."

"What were you doing in the swamps?" Safina asked. "I thought it was against the rules."

"Never mind why," Endera snapped. "Anyway, suddenly we heard a noise. I told Glorian and Nelly to get behind me."

Abigail stifled a giggle—Endera had pulled the two girls in front of her and hid behind them—but she remained silent.

"And that's when it came out of the woods. It was as tall as the ceiling, black as night, waving its arms around and saying—"

"Ooooooo," Abigail moaned, exactly as she'd done in the swamps.

Endera whirled, her face a mask of surprise. "Yes, that was the sound, but how did you—?"

Abigail threw her cloak over her head and waved her arms about as Calla did the same.

Endera's cheeks turned red as shreeks' eyes at night. "It was you. Very funny, Abigail. But you won't be laughing when I go straight to Madame Hestera and tell her what you did."

"Go ahead. And while you're at it, you can explain why you were out in the swamps. Safina is right—it's against the rules. We had permission from Madame Camomile to seek out a plant. What's your excuse?" She stepped in closer to Endera, her voice dropping. "And besides, we're witches, remember? We don't have to be nice to one another. Remember that cave on Jotunheim when you used a choking spell and left me to die? I haven't forgotten."

Endera's face leached of all color, and then without another word, she stomped her foot and left.

Glorian moved past her, keeping her distance. Her eyes were round with shock at Abigail's words, but Abigail was glad she'd said them. She was tired of Endera always throwing her weight around.

"Scare me like that again, and I'll skin you alive," Nelly hissed, waggling her sharpened nails at Abigail, before hurrying after the others.

"Did you really spook Endera like that?" Safina asked as the other firstlings hurried off to class.

"Yes. It was a bit mean."

"Well, like you said, witches aren't nice, are they?" Safina flashed her a grin and then hurried after the other girls.

"It's nice to see at least Safina's not mad at you anymore," Calla said. "You really laid into Endera. It's not like you, but maybe it needed to be said," she added quietly.

Abigail sighed, already regretting her harsh words. "We have a few minutes before class starts. Let's go find Madame Camomile and see if she can make a healing potion for Baba Nana. I have a feeling Capricorn's not going to wait long to start whatever she's planning."

They found Madame Camomile tinkering in her garden.

"Did you find some berries?" she asked, snipping away at the plants that lined her shelf.

"Yes." Abigail opened the small pouch, and the teacher beamed.

"Well done. Perfectly ripe. Calla, be a dear and boil some water. There's a kettle over there half-full."

Calla called up a ball of witchfire in her hand. She held the kettle over it while Madame Camomile fussed with the berries.

"Abigail, my mortar and pestle are on the shelf."

She fetched the utensils, and the teacher began to grind the fruit. The outsides were yellow, but the inside was a gooey orange that smelled like sulfur.

"Ugh." Abigail plugged her nose.

"I know. A rather strong odor." Madame Camomile scraped the paste into the teakettle and gave it a stir. "Take this straight to Baba Nana and pour her half a cup. No more, no less. Make sure she drinks it all."

"What if that doesn't work? Should we try again?"

"No. Too much and it acts like a poison. If this doesn't work, I'm afraid it might be nothing is ever going to bring her back."

"It's going to work," Calla said firmly, clutching the kettle. "Come on, Abigail, let's go."

They hurried out the door and down the hall toward Madame Vex's chambers, where Baba Nana was being kept. They were in such a hurry to find out if their potion worked that they didn't see the string that ran across the floor until it was too late.

Their boots caught, and both girls went flying. The kettle flew out of Calla's hands and hit the stone floor with a loud crash, sending the top flying and the precious liquid seeping out onto the stone.

"No!" Calla leaped up to right it.

"What happened?" Abigail rubbed at her stinging knees.

They turned to see a string stretched across the stairs leading to Madame Vex's chambers.

"Endera," they said in unison.

Tears clouded Calla's eyes as she looked into the kettle. "It's almost gone."

Abigail put a hand on her arm. "There's still some left."

"But Madame Camomile said we had to give her half a cup. There isn't enough and we picked all the berries off the bush."

"Doesn't matter. We still have to try."

Calla nodded, and they continued up the stairs. Abigail knocked, and the door was swiftly yanked open by Madame Vex.

"Well?" she demanded, looking down her thin nose at them.

"We have a potion that Madame Camomile helped us with," Abigail said.

Madame Vex peered inside the kettle. "There's hardly a few teaspoons."

"I know. We had an accident on our way."

She raised one brow but bade them come in.

Calla hurried to Baba Nana's side. The old witch lay on a small cot in the corner of the room. Her skin was tinged blue and Abigail could feel the cold radiating from her. The only sign of life was the slow rise and fall of her chest.

"She's nearly gone," Madame Vex said. "I don't know if anything will bring her back."

Calla knelt at her side as Abigail fetched a teacup from Madame Vex's cupboard.

"It has to work," Calla whispered. "I miss her too much."

Abigail poured the orangish liquid into the cup. It was well below the halfway mark, although the smell was still pungent. "Open her mouth."

Calla tugged down on the old witch's wrinkled chin, and Abigail held the cup to her lips, gently easing the liquid in. Baba Nana swallowed it with a sigh.

"That's all of it."

Abigail set the cup down and took Baba Nana's hand in hers. Her fingers were stiff and cold as icicles.

Madame Vex hovered nearby as they all held their breath. After a few moments, when nothing changed, her shoulders drooped. "I'm sorry, girls. It was worth a go. I'll leave you to say your goodbyes. She's not going to see many more sunrises."

The headmistress patted them both on the back and took her leave.

Calla's shoulders shook with sobs. "I don't want to say goodbye."

Abigail hesitated and then said, "There's one more thing we can try." She pulled the spellbook out of her bag. "I talked to Vertulious last night. He has a new healing spell."

"Wait, does it require you to use dark magic?"

Abigail bit her lip, then nodded.

"Then don't do it," Calla said in a choked whisper. "I know you hate what it does to you."

"But what if Baba Nana can help fix things? I don't have a choice."

Grimly, she opened the book and flipped through the pages. "Show me the healing spell," she commanded.

The pages flew past on their own and stopped. The writing on the page swam into focus, and a sliver of dread crawled down Abigail's back as an image of a wraith moved across the page. Vertulious was right—she'd looked through the spellbook many times and never seen this page. Setting the spellbook on the table, she cleared her throat and recited the words.

"*Spiritus, nefaria. Malfis animos.*"

Fire streaked through her veins as witchfire sprang to life in her hands.

She held the witchfire over Baba Nana's chest, and it spread out like a net, encasing the old hag in a glowing field of energy. A rush of wind picked up in the closed room and swirled their skirts around their knees. The shutters rattled on their hinges, and a glass fell to the floor, shattering.

Cold seeped into Abigail's bones as a deep dragging on her magic pulled her down into the darker side. The wound in her shoulder throbbed—she could feel warmth spread as blood oozed onto her clothes. A drop of it fell on the page of the open spellbook, and instantly her witchfire changed color, turning from green to blue to purple. Her blood sang at the use of power, and another part of her shrank back at the raw hunger for more it evoked.

After a few moments, Calla said, "That's enough."

Abigail tried to lower her hands, but they refused to obey her. A fissure opened inside her, unsealing a reservoir of magic she hadn't known was there. Her witchfire leaped in intensity and filled the room with purplish-green light. It wasn't until Calla forcibly pushed Abigail's hands down that the witchfire died out, leaving her heaving with exertion.

Calla knelt down and took Baba Nana's hand. "She's warming up!"

Color was returning to the old hag's cheeks. After a moment, her lips pursed, and then her eyes flew open. She took in the two of them staring at her.

"Calla," she croaked out. "Is that really you?"

"Yes, Baba Nana. Oh, you're back!"

Abigail placed a pillow behind the old witch's head and sat her up enough to drink from a glass of water. Baba Nana drank it down, smacking her lips with satisfaction.

"How long have I been asleep?"

"Long enough to miss all the action." Calla's eyes glowed as she clasped Baba Nana's hands. "There was almost a war, but Abigail and the others managed to stop it."

"What of Melistra?" Spite burned in Baba Nana's eyes. "I have a few things I'd like to say to her before I incinerate her."

"Melistra is gone." Abigail explained how Vertulious had been brought back and the price Melistra had paid.

"So that old alchemist tricked Rubicus—I can almost admire him for that," Baba Nana said.

"Except he wanted to bring war to Orkney. We managed to send him back into the spellbook." Abigail showed her the book.

Baba Nana shrank back. "It's dangerous to keep that."

"No. Vertulious's powers were drained during the battle. He's harmless now."

"But there's something wrong, isn't there?" Baba Nana studied their faces.

Abigail sighed. "We thought we'd fixed things by stopping the war. I tricked Vertulious into going back into the spellbook, and then I threw it into the sea to the mermaid queen."

Her eyes widened. "Tell me you didn't trust that lying sea witch?"

Shame washed through Abigail. "She promised to bury it deep in the ocean so it would never see the light of day again."

"But she lied." Baba Nana wrinkled her lips in disgust. "What did she want it for?"

"To use a spell to release Jormungand from his underwater prison."

The old witch paled, her fingers flying to her lips. "She didn't. Not even she is that reckless. That serpent can—"

"Destroy the world," Abigail finished. "Now you understand why we were so desperate to wake you. We need to know how to stop her. And how to get Jormungand back in his cage."

Baba Nana sank back against the pillows, her fingers plucking at the thin blanket. "A beast like that won't be tamed easily. It will have to be captured and dragged back."

"How will we find something strong enough to drag it? It's impossible," Calla wailed.

"Hush, girl, let me think. You'll have to give it a reason to return. Set a trap with bait it can't resist. I need to return to my shack immediately. I have books there that will help."

Abigail bit her lip. "If I miss another day of classes, I'll never get caught up."

"Don't worry about it," Calla said. "I'm ahead in every subject. You go to class, and I'll help Baba Nana. And thank you." She flung her arms around Abigail, whispering in her ear, "Be careful with that spellbook. I felt it's power—it was even darker than before. It frightens me."

Abigail's stomach grew queasy as she stored the book back in her bag. Calla was right, but she didn't want to think about it. She quickly left the room and hurried down the steps, then came crashing to a halt.

Endera stood in the corridor, her hands planted on her hips. She pointed at the stain on the stone floor. "Oops. I see someone made a mess."

Abigail stood trembling, fighting back the urge to call up a big ball of witchfire and plant it in the girl's face.

"Go ahead," Endera taunted. "Show me what the witch who's failing every subject has against one of the top witchlings in our class."

Plant the ball of witchfire in her face. Watch her squeal in pain. Do it, dark witch. You know you want to.

Abigail started at the sudden intrusion into her thoughts. "Quiet," she muttered.

Endera blinked. "Excuse me?"

"Nothing. Just get out of my way." She shoved the girl aside and hurried to class, fighting back the sick feeling in her stomach. That voice. It was just like when Vertulious had invaded her thoughts from inside the spellbook, only this voice didn't belong to Vertulious. Oddly, it had sounded a lot like her own voice, which made no sense—unless she was losing her mind and hearing things.

Abigail slid into her seat in Awful Alchemy, but her head spun as Madame Malaria put the witchlings through their lessons. The girls all knew transformation spells that could change pebbles into ladybugs and pieces of chalk into tasty mushrooms. How was Abigail ever going to catch up?

After class, she approached Madame Malaria.

"Abigail, I was surprised to see you in class yesterday," the teacher said with a sniff. "You were my star pupil earlier in the year."

"I'd like to make up the work I've missed."

She gave Abigail a skeptical look. "A monumental task with only a few weeks left in the term. As you saw today, the other girls have mastered several complex spells."

"I'm willing to do the work. Please."

Madame Malaria dropped a textbook in her hands. "Read this from cover to cover and be able to perform an advanced transformation by exams."

"But . . ." Abigail stared down at the thick book. "How am I ever going to learn all that in time?"

"Hmph. Perhaps you should have thought of that sooner."

The same scene repeated in every one of Abigail's classes. Madame Arisa gave her reams of Horrible Hexes to study. Even Madame Vex, who was pleased by the news Baba Nana had awoken, handed her stacks of math figures to complete.

"If you're serious about catching up, this is what is required," she said. "And tell that old witch I'll stop in and see her later. There is a meeting of the High Witch Council I must attend this afternoon."

By the time Abigail made it back to her room, her arms ached from carrying reams of make-up work. She dumped it all on her desk and slumped down on the bed, staring at the large pile. She would never be able to make up the work and stop Capricorn.

She had to face it.

She was as good as done as a witch.

Chapter 10

Hugo made his way toward the rear of the Tarkana gardens, where the weeds were overgrown. Carefully avoiding the spot where he and Abigail had once fallen through a hole into the dungeon, he approached a thick wall of brambles. He dropped to his knees, pushed aside a branch, and—trying not to snag his clothes—crawled forward on his belly. It was hard going, but he'd done it more than once and knew what to expect.

Light appeared ahead, and he emerged into a tiny clearing. After using his elbows to pull himself out of the brush, he got to his feet and dusted off his pants.

He'd discovered this place a few weeks ago while searching for the spot where Vertulious had planted his apple tree. At first Hugo had assumed the tree was in the swamps, but after searching high and low for it, he had tried his luck in the gardens. He knew every inch of the place from visiting Abigail so many times, so it had come as a shock when he'd almost walked straight into this bramble bush. His heart had leaped. He was certain the thicket had not been there in months prior.

When he'd tried hacking at the brambles, he'd grown even more excited—they'd resisted his every effort to part them. It was only when he'd gotten to his knees and dug into the dirt that he'd been able to shimmy underneath the protective barrier.

Kneeling down, he ran his hand over the green leaves of the small tree that grew in the center. It stood only as tall as his waist, but three bright and shiny apples hung from its slender limbs.

Temptation itched his palms. He wanted to take one and taste it. Of course he did. It was natural to be curious. But he'd made a promise to the god of thunder, Thor, that he would destroy it.

Or maybe Abigail had made the promise, the voice in his head reasoned. Had he really made any promises? He thought of all the good the apples could do. His hand wavered, brushing against the cool, firm flesh, and the fruit broke off. He stepped back in shock. The red apple lay on the ground, glinting in the sunlight.

"Hugo, you must destroy the tree," he said aloud, hoping to convince himself. He pulled a sawblade from his bag and pressed the blade against the trunk. Sweat popped up on his brow. He didn't want to, but he forced his hand to move.

The blade didn't even make a dent.

Hugo pressed harder, using both hands. He'd taken the saw from his father's shed, and he knew it had just been sharpened, but no matter how hard he tried, the blade wouldn't cut the wood.

Relief filled him. He'd tried. It must take powerful magic to destroy a tree like this.

A distant voice called his name. Abigail. They'd been so busy discussing the end of the world, and then being chased by wraiths and hunting Baba Nana's cure, he hadn't had time to tell her about his discovery. Maybe she would have an idea how to destroy it. He eyed the apple on the ground, then quickly scooped it into his pocket, telling himself it was just to show Abigail what he'd found. He crawled out from the tree's hiding place, brushing the twigs off his sleeves as he hurried back toward the jookberry tree.

Abigail stood waiting. She was muttering to herself, and then her hands went to her ears, as if she were trying to shut something out.

"Abigail, are you okay?"

She whirled, her face pale. "Fine. Where have you been?"

Now was the perfect time to tell her about the apple tree. "I was in the gardens." He reached for the apple in his pocket and began to speak, but Abigail cut him off with an irritated sigh.

"Not now Hugo, we have more important things to discuss. We made the potion, but Endera tripped us, and it spilled."

Sadness swept over him. He'd liked Baba Nana, even though she was a little scary at times. "So that's it then?"

"Not exactly. I—" She hung her head. "I used dark magic to bring her back."

"You what? But how?"

"Capricorn gave the spellbook back to me. We ran into her in the gardens after we left you yesterday. I didn't have a choice."

"Why was the queen of mermaids here?"

"She said she had to pay back her debt to me but I think she was meeting with Madame Hestera, plotting something terrible." Her voice broke, and he grabbed her arm.

"Are you okay?"

"Yes. I'm fine. I just . . . I just want this nightmare to be over."

Abigail was lying. Professor Markus, his Superior Senses teacher, had taught them simple tricks to read people by the little tells or signs they gave off and Abigail had an easy tell when she was avoiding the truth. Her eyes looked to the left and down instead of at him. "You know you can tell me anything."

"I said I'm fine." And then she clapped her hands over her ears, whispering, "Stop it."

Something was definitely wrong. "Stop what?"

Her head swiveled toward him, and for a second, he didn't recognize her, as if something was behind her eyes making them cold. "Stop asking me if I'm fine." Then as if a switch was thrown, her eyes softened, and she put a hand on his arm. "Sorry about that. I'm just . . . I have so much homework to catch up on. I don't know how I'll ever get it done."

"I said I'd help with Maths."

"Thanks, Hugo. You're a real friend." But as she said it, she winced, as if the words were painful.

The iron gate to the swamps opened with a creak, and Calla appeared, a happy look on her face.

"Oh, Abigail, I still can't believe we did it." She grabbed Abigail's hands and danced her in a circle. "Baba Nana is resting in her cottage. She's weak, but I think she's going to be good as new."

Hugo smiled. "I'm so happy for you."

Abigail stepped back from her embrace. "We need to know what Capricorn is planning."

Calla's smile faded. "How are we going to do that?"

"Madame Vex said there was a meeting of the High Witch Council today. We have to listen in. See what we can learn."

"Abigail, if we get caught, they'll throw us in the dungeons," Hugo said.

"Not *we*, Hugo. We can't smuggle a Balfin boy in. Calla, you help your great-aunt out on occasion, don't you?"

"Yes, I sometimes serve tea during their meetings."

"Then you'll appear with some tea, and when you open the door, I'll slip behind the curtain." The witches held their meetings in the Great Hall in front of a floor-to-ceiling curtain that hid the Great Mother spider from sight. "They won't even know I'm there. I'll stay until everyone is gone."

The witchling tapped her chin with her finger. "It might work."

"It has to. Hugo, go find Jasper. Tell him everything we know and see if he has any ideas. We'll meet up later tonight at Baba Nana's. Agreed?"

"Agreed," he said.

The two witchlings hurried away. It wasn't until they were out of sight that Hugo realized he hadn't told Abigail about the tree. His hand went to his pocket, circling the small globe there. He would tell her next time he saw her—and get her to explain why she was acting so strange.

Chapter 11

C alla and Abigail hurried to the kitchens, where Calla ordered the cook to make up a tea tray, pretending her great-aunt had requested it.

"But she said she didn't want to be disturbed," Cook said, flustered.

"Well, she changed her mind." Calla clapped her hands. "Hurry. You know how she gets."

The red-cheeked woman flung her apron up as she hurried to do Calla's bidding. She added boiling water to a teapot and scooped in heaping spoonfuls of bitter sycamore leaves, then slotted five cups and a plate of jookberry muffins on a tray in record time.

Calla gave her a small curtsy as Cook used her apron to wipe the sweat off her brow. Then the two witchlings took the servants' corridor toward the Great Hall, Abigail trailing slightly behind.

"Who are the other witches on the High Council?" Abigail asked. The witches were very secretive, and little was said of the work they did.

"Besides Madame Hestera, there are four other witches, each of them more powerful than the next. Melistra used to be one, and she was replaced with Madame Vex, which was a big honor. Then there's Ulondra—she's the nicest of them. Her daughter is Head Witchling of the fourthlings. Luciana is a master at hexes. Whatever you do, don't cross paths with her, unless you want to be sporting a sneevil's tail. I heard she did that to a witchling who spilled tea on her."

"And the fourth?"

Calla shivered. "Anarae. If she finds you, she'll incinerate you into a pile of ash. Stay away from her. Even my great-aunt is wary of her."

"What's so bad about her?"

Calla stopped outside the door to the chambers. "It's just a feeling. When you look into her eyes, there's a coldness there like I've never seen in any other witch." She nodded at Abigail to open the door.

Calla stepped through, motioning Abigail with her chin to move ahead.

Ducking behind the thick black curtain that ran up to the ceiling, Abigail made her way on her hands and knees along the dais until she could hear voices. She lifted the bottom of the curtain, pleased to see she was directly behind Madame Hestera's throne.

"Hestera, haven't we enough problems?" a voice asked. "We can't afford to lose another war."

"Ulondra, mind your words," Madame Hestera warned.

"I was only saying—"

A cup rattled as Calla let her presence be known.

"Silence," Hestera hissed. "Who's there? I asked not to be disturbed."

There were soft footsteps, and then Calla spoke. "Sorry, Great-Aunt Hestera. I thought . . . that is . . . you usually like sycamore tea for your High Council meetings. And Cook made fresh jookberry muffins."

"Be gone, girl. I don't want to be disturbed."

"But Cook went to all that trouble."

Hestera growled in her throat, then sighed. "Fine, since you're here, set the tray down, and then be gone."

Abigail saw Calla's feet move across the dais and heard the clanking of silver as she poured her aunt some tea, curtsied, and left.

Hestera waited for the sound of the door closing before she resumed. "Where were we?"

Abigail leaned in, holding her breath.

"Capricorn cannot be trusted," a low, husky voice hissed. "She's a jealous, bitter creature."

"With the most powerful creature in the world at her beck and call, Luciana. Need I remind you?" Madame Hestera said.

"What if she can't control him? It's too dangerous. She should be stopped," Ulondra said.

The witches all argued over one another until Madame Hestera rammed her cane into the ground. "Silence! Stop bickering like a bunch of firstlings. We cannot say no to Capricorn. The witches and the mermaids formed an alliance centuries ago. We share many bloodlines. Our magic is similar to theirs. We can use this to our advantage."

"How?" Luciana asked.

"Odin will never stand for it," Madame Hestera said. "That high-and-mighty god will be forced to take action. He'll be the one to stop Capricorn, not us."

"But won't he blame us?" Ulondra asked.

"Not if we are clever. Capricorn is a vain creature. She fancied herself goddess of the sea until Aegir spurned her for that wretched Ran. She's never forgiven him. Her jealousy blinds her, makes her weak."

"Then how do we come out of this ahead?" a new voice asked, dripping with ice. That must be Anarae.

Abigail was listening so hard she didn't notice the movement of air above her until a hairy appendage brushed against her cheek. She stifled a scream, rolling on her back to look up. She had forgotten all about the Great Mother. The spider hovered over her, mandibles working as it inched downward.

Abigail lay flat on the floor, trying not to scream. She couldn't use magic for fear of being discovered. Her breath locked in her chest. The spider put its face directly over hers. Was it going to eat her? Bite her head off?

And then that voice in her head called out: *Spera nae mora. Leave her.*

The spider hesitated, then scuttled away.

Abigail breathed a silent sigh of relief. She rolled back to the edge of the curtain. Madame Hestera was speaking.

"Capricorn intends to send a warning to Odin by ordering Jormungand to destroy one of the Orkadian's precious isles."

Abigail's heart dropped. *Destroy an isle? What if it was Garamond?* Robert's home island had been lovely the short time she had visited, and the people . . . What of them?

"Interesting," Anarae purred. "Which one? Garamond, I hope."

"No. She wants to send a message, not bring Odin's wrath down on her. It's a small island called Fenjoy, inhabited by a few scattered fishermen and seagulls."

"What can she possibly hope to accomplish?"

"Once she shows Jormungand's might, Capricorn intends to take the serpent to Odin's island—the part of Asgard we share with his ninth realm. As you well know, when Odin dragged these islands here, he left a small piece of Asgard that connects the two together but keeps us apart. She intends to demand he strip Aegir and Ran of their powers and make her sole goddess of the seas. If he doesn't, she'll use the force of the serpent to destroy the piece of Asgard here in Orkney."

Anarae scoffed. "A serpent has that power?"

"This is no ordinary serpent. If left unchecked, he can grow in length to encircle this entire world. A single thrash of his tail can cause great earthquakes. I believe he can destroy whatever he seeks to."

"Fine," Anarae agreed. "And just what do you think will happen if Capricorn destroys Odin's little island?"

"I believe she is hoping it will open a gateway to all of Asgard."

"She wants to tear down the walls of Valhalla?" Anarae's voice was tinged with shock and respect.

Abigail bit back a gasp. Valhalla was the sacred home of the gods. Mere mortals were not allowed to pass through the walls guarding it. Was this what Vor had meant when she had said the world might end?

"It would seem so," Hestera gritted out.

Anarae tittered icily. "Good. Let her destroy that place. Maybe we can be sent back to Midgard. Imagine what we could do set loose in the world of men."

"Exactly." Madame Hestera rapped her cane on the dais. "If Capricorn succeeds, we will grow in power along with her."

"And if she fails?" Anarae asked.

"We'll deny any involvement. Leave me now. We will reconvene on the morrow."

Abigail's heart clenched. What Capricorn was planning was madness. The witches began to depart, but Madame Hestera called out, "Madame Vex, a word."

She waited for the other High Witches to depart before dropping her voice. "Madame Vex, we cannot let Capricorn drag us into this mess."

The headmistress stuttered. "B-but you said—"

Hestera rapped her cane again. "I can't afford to look weak in front of the High Witch Council, but if Capricorn fails, Odin's wrath on us will be unstoppable. We must look as if we've done our part. We'll send a warning message to Odin." Her voice dripped with contempt. "As much as I hate the thought. We cannot be seen as betraying our allies, nor can we be seen as aiding our greatest enemy's enemy."

"What would you have me do?"

"Send your most powerful witchling with this message." She passed a rolled-up scroll to the headmistress. "Choose an older girl. One who is discreet and can be trusted. She will need a map. You know the one I speak of."

"I will retrieve it from the archives. You have my word. It will be done."

Madame Hestera sighed, and her bones creaked as she

stood from her throne. "I am getting too old for all this intrigue," she muttered.

Their footsteps echoed across the marble floor, and finally the Great Hall was empty.

Abigail let out a sigh of relief and climbed out from underneath the curtain. Her legs trembled as she slipped out the side door into the servants' corridor—where she ran smack into Madame Vex. The headmistress was waiting with arms folded, still holding the rolled-up scroll.

"I thought I heard two sets of footsteps when Calla entered. What were you doing listening in?"

Abigail's heart thudded painfully in her chest. "Please, Madame Vex, don't tell."

"Why should I not report you to Madame Hestera?"

"Because she'll get rid of me for good this time. Let me take the message to Odin."

Madame Vex clutched the scroll tighter. "I can't entrust a mission like this to a second-year student. I have a witchling in mind. A sixth-year student, top of her class."

"But none of this would have happened if not for me."

"Exactly why I won't be sending you. Besides, if you leave now, your dream of being a witch will be over. You will fail all your classes and be expelled from the Tarkana Witch Academy. Madame Hestera will strip you of your magic."

Abigail's mind raced. "What if I caught up on all my work? Then I could take my exams when I get back."

"Impossible. You're too far behind. That's my final answer. Now leave me before I change my mind and report you to Madame Hestera."

Endera climbed down from the web behind the dais, gingerly skirting the massive spider. Having been to the netherworld, which was overrun with the things, she had a strong aversion to the creatures. But since her mother was gone, the only way to know what was going on in the coven was by eavesdropping. She'd taken to hiding in the corner of the web, careful not to be seen.

She'd had to stifle a gasp when she'd seen Abigail sneak in behind the curtain. She'd dearly wished for the Great Mother to eat her whole, but something had scared the spider off.

Endera sat down on Hestera's throne, swinging her legs, missing her mother. She would take her place on the High Council one day, and then everyone would know her mother's death hadn't been in vain. Hestera wanted someone to take a message to Odin. Endera would make sure she was the one to take it. The coven leader wanted an older student—but after failing to retrieve Thor's hammer back in Jotunheim, Endera knew she had to make up for it to earn the respect of the old hag she intended to replace one day.

Chapter 12

Abigail eyed the stack of work that needed completing, groaning. She slumped back onto her bed. It was too much. Even if she stayed up all night, she had missed weeks of classes. There were too many spells to memorize and too many math sheets to fill in. She buried her face in her hands.

"I can't do it," she whispered.

I can, that new voice whispered back.

Abigail shook her head. "I don't know who you are, but I can't listen to you."

I am you, dark witch.

"Stop calling me that."

But you like it. You know you do. We are powerful together. Powerful enough to tackle Jormungand.

Abigail raised her head. "What do you mean?"

Open the spellbook.

Abigail hesitated, then opened the cover. Mist began to rise and coalesce until a slender figure hovered over her bed. It was a mirror image of Abigail, only her eyes looked more sunken, her cheeks sharper, her lips pulled tight.

Abigail frowned. "I don't understand. Who are you?"

"Call me Abignus. I am your dark magic come to life. When you used the spellbook, you released me. You waste our time studying this nonsense"—she waved a hand at the pile of schoolwork—"when the spellbook contains more knowledge than all the books in this school."

"But I'll never be seen as a witch if I don't finish my schooling."

"Then let me help us."

"But what about Vertulious?"

Abignus dismissed him with a wave of her hand. "His powers are withered. I control the spellbook now."

Abigail chewed on her bottom lip. Everything about this was wrong. Vertulious had said the spellbook had a new master. It could be dangerous to even open it. But if she didn't get caught up, she would never become a great witch.

Temptation tugged at her. She could always toss the book into the fire if it became too bothersome.

She took a breath and then nodded. "So what do I do?"

"Turn the pages until I say stop."

Abigail riffled through the pages until the voice called a halt.

The words on the page burned in her brain before she could look away. She hesitated, fearing what the spell would do, but she needn't have bothered, because her wispy twin spoke the words for her.

"Facilitus, emeritus, cranius, maximus."

The pages of work on the desk stirred as if a breeze were passing through an open window. They rose over her head and began spinning and twirling. Light burned across the pages as words and numbers filled in. Her Awful Alchemy book opened, and words tumbled into her head—spell after spell being stored away. It was dizzying and sickening, and she couldn't make it stop.

But it was working.

Pages began to land in a neat stack on the table, the answers neatly penciled in with Abigail's handwriting. The Horrible Hexes book opened next, and she eagerly awaited the learning. History followed, filling her head with a boring list of dates and famous witch names, followed by Magical Maths. Lastly, Fatal Flora poison and plant names were etched into her brain as the last page fluttered down on her desk.

"That was amazing," Abigail whispered. Her head reeled with all the information she'd packed into it.

There was a soft knock on her door. Abigail slammed the spellbook shut, and the wispy figure vanished as Calla slipped inside.

"Well, what did you learn?" Her eyes went to all the finished stacks of papers, and her jaw dropped. "Abigail, you did all this work? I was going to help you."

"Never mind my schoolwork." Abigail shoved the papers in her book bag. "I know what Capricorn is planning."

"How bad is it?"

"Bad. She plans to send Jormungand to a small island to the north called Fenjoy."

"Fenjoy?" Calla's brows furrowed. "I've never heard of it."

"It's a small fishing island. She plans to destroy it to send a message to Odin."

"But won't innocent people lose their lives?"

"Not if we stop her," Abigail said firmly.

"So what do we do?"

"Hope Baba Nana has come up with some way to stop Jormungand."

Chapter 13

Hugo was late getting to the docks to see Jasper. His brother, Emenor, had collared him outside of town and dragged him home for supper. Then he'd had to do his homework *and* Emenor's in exchange for his brother saying nothing when he snuck out, so it was nearly dark by the time he slipped onto the deck of Jasper's rickety boat.

This time the old sailor didn't appear behind him with a knife, ready to cut his throat. Hugo lifted the latch and stuck his head in. "Hello? Jasper?"

A sound rustled below.

"Jasper? Are you there?"

There was a sharp rasp as someone struck flint, lighting a candle.

Jasper sat at the small galley table, his weathered face lined with worry. "What are you doing here, boy?"

"I came to ask for your help. You know about Jormungand?"

Jasper nodded. "I am a son of the sea. I know everything that happens in these parts."

"Then you know he has to be stopped."

"I know that mermaid queen is using him to do her bidding."

"And?"

Jasper's hand slammed down on the table. "Thanks to you and that blue witch, I owe Capricorn a favor."

The old sailor had made a bargain with the mermaids for safe passage when he had taken Hugo and Abigail to Jotunheim.

"If I set foot out on those waters, she will call on it, and I will have to obey. That is the price for her help."

"But—"

"No buts. I can't help you, lad. If I do, I'll lead you straight to your doom. Now take yourself and go before I toss you overboard myself."

Hugo reluctantly left, hopping down onto the dock and studying the other ships. There was a small warship loading supplies. Maybe they could steal it. He wandered closer, but there were too many Balfin soldiers moving about.

Sighing, he cut through the lower part of town and headed toward Baba Nana's cottage. When he heard voices and saw flickering light from a ball of witchfire, he quickened his pace.

"Surprise!" he yelled, jumping out in front of Abigail and Calla.

Calla squealed and nearly hurled the witchfire in his face. She relaxed once she recognized him. "Hugo, don't scare us like that. I could have incinerated you."

"Sorry. I have bad news. Jasper won't help. He's worried Capricorn will call in her favor and he'll be forced to betray us."

Abigail threw her hands up. "Then how will we get to Fenjoy in time to stop Capricorn from destroying it?"

"Fenjoy?" Hugo listened as Abigail explained what she'd learned in the High Council meeting. "So Capricorn wants all of Aegir's powers, and Ran's too, or else she's going to try and destroy his island?"

"Yes. If she does that, then all of Asgard is in danger, even the home of the gods."

"But that's impossible." Calla's eyes were wide.

"Not for that sea monster."

"What about Big Mama?" he asked.

Abigail shook her head. "She just had three new hatchlings. She won't leave them for long. We'll have to find another way."

They continued walking toward Baba Nana's cottage.

"Maybe Baba Nana will have good news," Hugo offered, but Abigail looked glum. "If you're worried about your schoolwork, I can help you study for Maths."

"No need," Abigail said quickly. "I found a way to get caught up."

"You used magic, didn't you?" Calla glanced at her sideways. "That's cheating."

"It's not cheating—it's called being a witch," Abigail said, but her cheeks were bright red, and Hugo could see the shame in her eyes.

"Where did you get a spell to do your homework for you?" Then it hit him. "You used the spellbook. I thought you hated Vertulious."

"Vertulious isn't the one helping me. It's . . . never mind. It doesn't matter. I didn't have a choice. I had to get caught up or face being expelled. So I did what I had to do, and if you don't like it, I don't care."

Her voice rose with each word until she was practically shouting. Hugo had never seen her so angry. Even her eyes looked a shade darker than normal.

He touched her arm. "You know that spellbook is full of dark magic."

"What's your point?"

Calla joined in. "Our point is that it changes you. Every time you use it."

"So what? If I become a stronger witch, what does it matter? We have to stop Capricorn. No matter the cost. We can't fail."

"It matters because of who you are here." Hugo pointed at her chest where her heart lay. "And if you can't see that, maybe it's too late."

"Maybe you don't know everything, Hugo Suppermill." Her eyes grew bright with tears, and she hurried on ahead of them down the narrow track.

"You think she'll be okay?" Calla asked.

Hugo sighed. "I think that spellbook is bad news. But unfortunately, we might need it to survive this."

"Even if it costs Abigail her soul?"

"We won't let that happen," he said firmly. "Come on, let's see if Baba Nana has news for us."

Chapter 14

Abigail angrily scrubbed the tears away. What was the point of crying anyway? A witch's heart was made of stone. She didn't care what Hugo thought, or Calla for that matter.

Your friends make you weak, Abignus whispered in her head.

"Oh, just be quiet," Abigail said, glad to see Baba Nana's shack. Smoke rose from the chimney. She pushed open the rickety door and found the old witch huddled over some journals on her table, studying them in the light of a small oil lantern.

Baba Nana quickly covered the books with her cloak until she saw who it was, and then her face sagged in relief. "It's you. I thought perhaps . . ."

"Thought what?" Abigail asked, moving closer.

"Nothing. Madame Vex said she might stop by." She let out a long coughing wheeze, dabbing her mouth with a rag. "Curse that Melistra," she said once she'd recovered. "It's going to take a long while for me to be on my feet."

Abigail sat and turned one of the books toward her. "What is this?"

Calla and Hugo entered and sat down on either side of her. "I've never seen these before," Calla said, flipping through the pages of one. "They look like diaries."

"These are Vena Volgrim's journals."

Vena was one of the ancient witches who had been set into stone after she and her sister Catriona went to war one too many times with mankind, leading Odin to send all creatures of magic into this corner of his ninth realm of Asgard.

"But you said they were destroyed after the coven blamed you, not Melistra, for creating the viken," Abigail said.

The old witch sighed. "I lied. I never wanted to open these cursed pages again. But needs-be. Here we are."

"Have you found something that will help us catch the serpent?" Hugo asked.

Her face lightened. "Vena encountered Jormungand. She used to visit him in his prison cell underwater. She enjoyed studying him. I think she was hoping to create a creature like him of her own."

Baba Nana turned the journal around. There was a sketch of a large stone enclosure with rugged walls and a dark pool in the center. The drawing was very detailed and precise. Iron bars lined one side of the cage, and beyond them, the head of a serpent could be seen rising out of the water as if to strike.

"He looks . . . angry," Abigail said.

"As he should. He's been locked up for centuries," Baba Nana said.

"How does this help us?" Calla asked.

"I'm not sure. Vena wrote in her notes that the only time Jormungand would let her near him was when she brought him a rare delicacy, a horrible-smelling fruit known as borakora. The serpent couldn't resist it, and she was able to get close enough to study him."

"Where can we find some?" Abigail asked.

"Madame Camomile might have some in her greenhouse. There's a popular stink bomb potion she peddles."

"I'll ask her for some first thing," Calla said. "I can tell her it's for my great-aunt."

"Once you've set a trap, you'll need chains strong enough to lead him back to his prison," Baba Nana said.

Abigail wanted to groan. "Where are we going to find chains like that?"

Hugo piped in. "Odin had some made when he led Jormungand there."

"So add finding Odin's chains to our list," Abigail said with a sigh. "Thank you, Baba Nana. This is very useful."

Calla wrapped her arms around the old witch. "I'm so glad you're back."

The witch chuckled. "I hope I'm never cold again." Then her face grew serious as Calla stepped back. "Be careful, all of you. One nick of that serpent's venomous fangs and your heart would stop."

Abigail stood. "We should go. It's late, and if we get caught sneaking in, Madame Vex will throw us in the dungeons."

"Yes. We need to pack and get ready for our next adventure," Hugo said, grinning at her.

Your friends will let you down, Abignus warned.

Abigail resisted the urge to clasp her hands over her ears and instead hurried out, practically racing down the path.

Hugo caught up to her, grabbing her by the arm. "Abigail, stop."

She froze, staring straight ahead.

"I'm sorry," he said.

"We both are," Calla added as she joined them. "I shouldn't have said you were cheating."

"Wasn't I?" Abigail said, biting back bitter tears.

"It doesn't matter," Calla replied. "We're your friends. We're here for you."

Abigail nodded, feeling the thorn in her chest ease. She drew in a deep breath. "I know, and I'm sorry. About earlier. I shouldn't have got so mad."

The witchlings said goodbye to Hugo and hurried through the woods, using a small ball of witchfire to light their way. They quickly scrambled up the ivy to Abigail's attic window and eased their way inside.

Calla had said nothing the entire way home, but now she walked over to the bed and lifted the spellbook, running her hand over the cover. "It's changing, isn't it?"

"What do you mean?"

Calla dropped it back on the bed, as if she found it distasteful, and shrugged. "I don't know. It feels different, and not in a good way."

Abigail forced a yawn. "I have a big day tomorrow. I have to finish catching up so I don't get expelled."

Calla smiled, but it didn't reach her eyes. She put a hand on Abigail's arm. "You'll let me know if it gets to be too much?"

Abigail laughed. "It's fine. Really. Nothing I can't handle."

"But you'll tell me if it is. Promise?" She stared intently into Abigail's eyes.

Abigail smiled, crossing her fingers behind her back. "Promise."

Chapter 15

Madame Vex shuffled through the stacks of homework Abigail had handed her. It was every assignment due in all of her classes. The headmistress frowned as she read through the work to the end, then raised shocked eyes to study Abigail. "How did you complete all this in one night?"

Abigail forced herself to yawn. "I stayed up all night. I know you told me I can't go, but I have to find a way to stop Capricorn."

"What is it you think a witchling like you can do about it?"

"I don't know. Yet. But I always think of something."

She studied Abigail with a piercing gaze. "And you've memorized all of your assigned spells and hexes?"

Abigail nodded.

"Memorized Madame Camomile's Fatal Flora list?"

Abigail recited the top ten poisonous plants and where to find them. It was strange being able to call up such knowledge, and she exulted in it.

"And you stayed up all night?" The headmistress's voice dripped with skepticism.

Abigail clasped her hands, wavering between telling the truth and lying. "I might have used a little magic to help," she finally confessed, hoping that wouldn't earn her a failing grade.

Instead, Madame Vex's eyes sparkled. "Magic, you say? It must have been very powerful. I'm pleased, Abigail. A witch should use whatever they have at their disposal. You've proven to be a very resourceful witchling. I can't approve of your little venture, but if anyone asks where you are, I'll tell them you've had a setback and will be ready for final exams. I suggest you don't miss them."

"If I do, it will be because Jormungand swallowed me," Abigail said, earning a smile from Madame Vex.

She raced up the steps to the dormitory tower, eager to pack a few things in a satchel and meet Calla in the gardens. She opened the door to her room and gasped in shock.

Someone was there already—a witch with high cheekbones and eyes that were such a dark green they might have been black. Thick raven-colored hair was coiled atop her head, making her appear taller.

"Abigail, there you are."

Abigail recognized that cold voice. It was Anarae, the High Witch Calla had described as the coldest of them all.

Abigail curtsied. "How may I help you?"

"Do you know who I am?"

"You're Madame Anarae, one of the High Witches."

The witch tilted Abigail's chin with one finger, the nail tipped in black lacquer. "I am curious about you. Show me your witchfire."

Abigail obediently called up a ball of green witchfire, but Anarae *tsked* in annoyance.

"I'm not a fool. Your real witchfire. I've heard the rumors about you."

Abigail slowly slipped the sea emerald from around her neck and dropped it in her pocket. Then she rubbed her fingers together and a small ball of blue witchfire appeared.

Anarae's eyes widened. "Fascinating." She put her hand over Abigail's to feel the power in the witchfire, and then it winked out. "You were there, lurking behind the curtain yesterday, weren't you?"

Abigail gulped but kept her silence.

"Don't bother to answer. I like a witchling who goes after what she wants. It could be useful to have another set of eyes and ears. Perhaps you would like to be my protégé. I could take you under my wing."

Abigail's eyes bulged. "I mean . . . that would be a great honor. But I'm afraid I can't."

Say yes, the voice in her head clamored. *She will give us great powers.*

Annoyance and surprise passed over the witch's face. "You're saying no? To a High Witch?"

"No . . . I'm sorry. It's just I'm . . ." Abigail stopped herself, suddenly flooded with doubt. What was she doing? Setting off on another adventure that was sure to get her killed, and if not that, then kicked out of the coven.

Stay and grow our powers, Abignus urged. *Be the dark witch you know you are.*

Abigail pasted on a smile. "I'm flattered. It's just I've missed so many classes I'm behind. Can I . . . that is . . . may we begin when the term is over?"

The irritation on Anarae's face smoothed. "Excellent idea. Finish your classes, and the summer will be ours for getting to know each other and exploring your talents. I think you will be very useful to this coven."

A black cloud enveloped the High Witch, and she was gone.

Abigail expelled the breath she'd been holding and swiftly gathered her things into a small bag, along with the spellbook.

Calla was waiting in the gardens. She opened her bag and showed Abigail the prickly green fruit inside. It was the size of a bread loaf and smelled faintly of rotting garbage. "Madame Camomile wasn't happy to part with it. Said I was costing her plenty in stink bomb potions, but I said my aunt needed it desperately."

They made their way quickly down to the docks. Hugo stood outside Jasper's ship. There was no sign of movement on board.

"Is he in there?" Abigail asked.

Hugo shrugged. "I think so."

"Let me handle this."

She ducked under the railing and dropped her bag on the deck, then went to the hatch and pulled it open. The galley was dim, but she could make out the shadowy figure seated at the table.

"Jasper, I'm coming down," she said.

The old sailor stared glumly at a mug he cradled with both hands. "I already told your Balfin friend I can't help you."

"I know. But I'm here to change your mind."

"Blue Witch, I'm not going to betray you," Jasper said gruffly.

"It's not a betrayal if we know why you're doing it, is it?"

He scowled. "I suppose not."

"Capricorn is planning on using Jormungand to destroy Fenjoy and send a message to Odin. His island of Asgard is next."

Jasper's brow furrowed. "Fenjoy's a miserable spit of land. There's only a couple dozen folk that live there, mostly old fishermen."

"She's going to destroy it," Abigail pressed. "If we don't do something to stop her. I can't let that happen, even if it is just a few old fishermen. We have to put an end to this or Asgard is next, and that could be very bad."

He grunted. "Good luck finding Asgard. Odin's island changes location all the time. One minute it's before you, and the next it's hidden away across the sea."

"Capricorn knows all the sea creatures. What if she can track it? Look, I'd ask Big Mama to fly us, but she just had a new batch of hatchlings."

"If I take you out on the open waters, that sea witch will call on my favor to take you straight to her."

"If you don't take us, who will stop her? We have to get to Fenjoy in time to warn them."

He grunted again. "I suppose you're right."

"So you'll do it?"

He nodded reluctantly.

"Good. After Fenjoy, we'll head to Asgard. Hestera is sending a witchling to warn Odin."

"Playing both sides, is she?"

Abigail nodded.

"She's a fool then. A witch can't penetrate the island's defenses. Only someone with the blood of Odin can do that." He stood. "You stay below out of sight. Don't need anyone asking questions about witchlings on board."

He disappeared up the steps, and a moment later Calla bounded down, closing the hatch behind her.

Her eyes glowed. "I can't believe I'm going on an adventure like this."

The floor tilted under their feet as the ship moved away from the dock.

Abigail smiled faintly. "It won't be easy. Capricorn could call in Jasper's favor at any time, and he could be forced to toss us overboard."

But Calla's enthusiasm wasn't dented. "Maybe I'll see my mom."

"Do you think she'll be on our side?"

"Of course. She's a witch first. At least, I think she is." Calla's eyes grew troubled.

They sat in silence a few minutes.

This witchling will betray us, the voice in Abigail's head whispered.

Abigail bit down on her cheek to stop herself from responding. "Calla, we're going to have to confront the mermaids at some point, and that will mean going in the water."

"I'll be okay. I can fight it. I think. I don't want to be a mermaid." She raised her eyes to Abigail. "I'm a witch through and through." But her voice wavered, and Abigail could tell she was frightened.

When she betrays us, it will be the end.

Abigail dug her fingernails into her palm. "Let's go see if we are out of the harbor. I need some fresh air." And a chance to get away from that incessant voice. Honestly, it was worse than when Vertulious had been haunting her. It was as if she was haunting herself, and she didn't know how to stop it.

Hugo waved at them as they opened the hatch, and Abigail's heart lightened. Her friend was so brave and true.

He's a Balfin. He is weaker than us. Use him as needed but don't trust him.

And just like that, her spirits drooped. Because that voice was like poison dripping into her veins.

Hugo waved them out. "Come see. Jasper's put up some new sails."

Abigail tilted her head back, eyeing the fresh canvas. "Nice."

"They won't last long," Jasper muttered. "They never do. The winds out here tear 'em apart."

"What a beautiful day." Calla spun in delight. "The water is so blue." She bent over the rail and trailed her hand along the surface.

Jasper shouted, "Don't touch the water here. We're too close."

She snatched her hand back. "Why not? Are there mermaids here?"

"Not mermaids." He eyed the water warily. "The *akkar.*"

"What's the akkar?" Abigail asked, but at that moment, a swell moved the ship abruptly to the side, nearly knocking her off her feet.

A long tentacle shot out of the water, and then a massive, bulbous gray head bobbed to the surface. A single yellow eye blinked at them. On the other side of the ship, another head popped up, then another, until they were surrounded by these enormous tentacled beasts.

"That's the akkar," Jasper announced. "Guardians of Balfour Island."

"How come I've never seen one before?" Hugo cried as another tentacle shot out, slapping the water next to them.

"Because I'm careful not to alert them," Jasper growled. He grabbed a long spear from a rack by the mast. "They'll tear this boat to pieces if we don't stop them. Hugo, take the wheel. I'll try to scare them off."

Jasper stood on the prow of the boat, his arm cocked. His long gray hair fluttered in the breeze. As the akkar raised its tentacle to strike, Jasper threw his spear and hit it in the center of its eye. It let out an angry squeal, and gray blood sprayed, covering the surface of the sea in an oily slick. The other two wrapped their tentacles around the ship. One thick arm crashed down on the deck, but Hugo was there to stab at it with a kitchen knife. Calla and Abigail threw witchfire that sputtered out on its thick skin. But neither was enough to make the akkar withdraw. In moments, their ship was going to be nothing more than driftwood.

Before she could think better of it, Abigail pulled the spellbook out of her bag and stared down at the cover.

Dark witch, yes, let's do this.

Calla put her hand on it. "No, Abigail. Let's try something else first."

"Like what?"

"Come on, you learned every spell. Think of one."

Abigail's mind raced. The ship jolted under their feet as another tentacle crashed down next to Hugo.

"Hurry," he shouted, stabbing at it with his knife. Jasper wrestled with it, pushing it overboard.

"Lightning spell," she said.

Calla nodded. "I know that one. Together."

Planting their feet on the deck, they murmured the words in unison. "*Fulmen ignus.*" Flinging their hands at the closest akkar, a sharp jagged bolt of lightning shot out of their hands, striking its bulbous head. It squealed with rage but continued its attack on the ship.

"It's not working," Calla said.

"Abigail, help!" Hugo's shout came from behind them. He dangled in the air, wrapped up in a tentacle. Jasper flung his last spear at the appendage, but it went wide.

Desperate, Abigail opened the pages of the spellbook. "Show me a spell."

We'll use your spell only we'll make it better, Abignus purred. The pages flipped forward and then stopped.

Abigail didn't hesitate. Raising her hand, she recited the words. "*Fulmen ignus corsuscatio.*"

A strange power reverberated through her like a shock wave, and then a bolt of green lightning shot out of her hands, striking the akkar holding Hugo. It let out a squealing roar of pain, dropping Hugo back onto the deck. She directed a burst at another bobbing form. Power surged in her, thrumming in her veins and making her heart pound. She sent a third bolt, and this time the gray figures sank from sight.

Chest heaving, she rushed to Hugo's side.

"Are you okay?"

"Fine. What was that magic?"

"Aye, I've never seen anything like it," Jasper said, lifting Hugo to his feet. They waited for her answer.

"Abigail used the spellbook," Calla said.

"I saved us," Abigail said defensively.

That's right. You did what you had to, Abignus whispered in her ear.

"But at what cost?" Hugo asked. "Every time you use that spellbook, it's like you lose a piece of yourself."

"What is your point?" Abigail said, feeling her temper rise. "I am a witch. Do you get that? A witch, and I will do whatever it takes to get what I want."

"And what is it you want?" Hugo shouted, surprising her with his anger. "To be awful like Melistra? I thought you were different."

"Melistra was a powerful witch who went after what she wanted. What's wrong with wanting that?"

"Nothing," Calla said calmly. "If you were like every other witch in the coven. It's just not who you are. You care too much about things."

"Maybe you don't know me at all," Abigail snapped. "And you're welcome, all of you, for saving your life." She stomped down below deck, slamming the hatch behind her.

She huddled on a bunk, her arms wrapped around her knees as tears cascaded down her cheeks, trying to ignore the crowing voice in her head that was so thrilled with what she'd done.

Chapter 16

ndera was like a shadow, following Madame Vex's
every movement. She needed that scroll, but she
didn't want Madame Vex to know she'd taken it.
She had to discover who the headmistress was giving it to
and then convince that witchling it was in her best interest
to hand it over.

As she hid behind some long curtains that lined the
hallway outside Madame Vex's chambers, Endera grew
stiff and cold as the hours passed. But just when she was
about to give up for the night, she heard the rasp of a
footstep and peered out. A witchling was approaching,
her face pinched with worry. She clutched a small satchel
in one hand. Endera racked her brain and came up with
the witchling's name: a sixthling named Solara. The older
girl's powers would be greater than her own.

Endera gritted her teeth. She would just have to be
convincing.

Solara raised her hand and knocked softly. The door
opened immediately, and Madame Vex pulled the girl
inside, poking her head out to check the hall.

As soon as the door closed behind them, Endera stepped past the curtain, shook out her stiffness, and hurried back down the hallway, certain now of her prey. She made her way to the gardens and cupped her hand to her face, letting out the sharp call of a nightwing bird.

After a moment, there was an answering call that sounded more like a cat wallering, but Endera took it as a sign the others were ready.

Hiding behind some bushes, she waited. It took about ten minutes, and then footsteps sounded on the paving stones in the garden.

Solara had her cloak wrapped around her and was hurrying toward the gate that led out of the gardens. Endera fell into step behind her, biding her time.

The witchling opened the gate to the path that led to Jadewick, and Endera picked up her pace, drawing closer. At one point the girl turned around, and Endera faded back into the shadows, then resumed following when Solara continued on.

As they approached the edge of town, Endera whistled sharply.

There was a rustling sound and then a low growl.

Solara froze as a Shun Kara wolf stepped out of the woods.

"Stay away," she said, backing up and drawing a ball of witchfire.

The Shun Kara ignored it, dragging one meaty paw in the dirt, and snarled a warning.

"Careful, or he'll tear you apart before you launch that puny ball of witchfire," Endera said, announcing her presence.

Solara turned, relief crossing her face. "Endera, right? Is this beast a pet of yours?"

Endera snapped her fingers, and the shaggy wolf sat on its haunches. "Damarius listens to me. When it pleases him. I'll take that scroll." She held out her hand.

Solara's face tightened, and her arm went protectively around the satchel she carried. "This is none of your business. A secondling has no chance of sailing to Asgard."

"And yet, it is exactly what I'm going to do." Endera sauntered closer, leaning in to whisper, "Unless you'd like to see what he can do."

Damarius growled, showing his teeth.

Solara's hands flashed, and twin balls of witchfire appeared over her palms. She aimed quickly, lobbing one at Damarius and the other at Endera.

Endera ducked, dropping to all fours, but Damarius squealed as the shot landed. The creature rolled on the ground to put out the witchfire.

Solara called two more, stepping confidently forward to hover over Endera. "Give it up, secondling. Don't make me use these."

Two shadows slunk out of the trees, and then Glorian and Nelly tackled the older witchling, knocking the witchfire from her hands as she landed hard on the ground. Glorian sat on top of her, holding her down, while Nelly pinned her arms. Endera tugged the satchel from her.

"How were you planning on traveling?" she demanded.

Solara snarled at her. "I'll never tell you. Madame Vex is going to have you expelled."

"No, because you're not going to tell her what happened. You're going to say you got scared and chanced upon me, and I offered to go in your place."

"Why would I do that?"

"Because you made Damarius mad."

The wolf lunged at the girl, snapping his teeth an inch from her face.

Solara shrank back. "There's a ship. The captain is supposed to take me to Asgard."

"What about the map?" Madame Hestera had said something about a special map to Madame Vex. "You have it?"

The girl hesitated then as Damarius growled louder, she nodded.

"How does it work?" Endera asked.

"The ink was penned with the blood of a son of Odin. It can guide us there. I swear, Endera, if you do this and fail, it will be on my head."

Endera grinned. "I know. Isn't that grand? Tie her up," she said to Nelly.

Nelly pulled out a length of rope, and she and Glorian tied the witchling to the nearest tree.

"I'll make you pay for this." Solara's eyes smoldered with hatred. "I will have every sixthling in the coven after you."

"Bring it, Solara. I welcome the challenge."

Endera stood and turned away, snapping her fingers at the others to follow.

Her heart was racing as they made their way to the docks. She had done it! Now all she had to do was find Asgard and deliver the scroll.

"Are you sure about this, Endera?" Glorian asked. "We could get in loads of trouble."

"I'm sure that I'm going to claim the glory. If you don't want to come along, stay. It's not like I need you."

Nelly snorted. "Where's the fun in going to Asgard to deliver a message to a god if there's no one with you to see you do it?"

Endera's step lightened. Nelly was right. Not that she was scared to go alone, but she would enjoy the moment all the more when her friends watched her triumph.

They arrived at the harbor, and she scanned the darkened warships. Only one had a lantern burning. She walked briskly across the gangplank and landed lightly on the deck. The captain whirled around, and his face shifted to one of shock when he saw her.

"You," he spat.

Sudden rage boiled over inside her. It was the same captain who had left Endera and her companions to die on the frozen river of Jotunheim.

Witchfire sprang to her hands. "Get off," she commanded.

"This is my ship," he barked. "If you throw that witchfire you risk burning the entire ship."

She let the witchfire go out, giving a low whistle.

Behind her, Damarius leaped on board, snarling and tearing at the former captain's pants. He raced for the side of the ship, swiftly leaping overboard, landing in the water with a splash. The Shun Kara turned to growl at the rest of the crew, daring them to do something. They held back warily.

"Who is second-in-command?"

A younger man stepped forward. "I'm second-in-command."

"Good. You're the captain now. Take me to Asgard."

He hesitated. "No disrespect, witchling, but Asgard is impossible to find."

"Then it's a good thing I have a map." She pulled a folded square out of the satchel and tossed it to him. "Set sail."

He grinned. "Aye, aye, witchling."

Chapter 17

After the attack by the akkar, the day at sea passed uneventfully. Abigail couldn't stay sulking below, it was too stuffy in the airless cabin, so she went back top and took a position at the front of the boat. The others pretended like nothing had happened which suited her just fine. Hugo helped Jasper with the rigging on the boat and relieved the sailor at the helm. Calla kept staring out at the water as if she were searching for something, maybe a sign her mother was nearby.

Abigail scoured the spellbook, looking for a way to control Jormungand and get him back in his prison. There were several new spells she was certain she had never seen before, but nothing that helped her solve her problem. She put the book down, laying back and closing her eyes. Maybe Hugo was right. Maybe turning to the spellbook for help every time was a mistake. She had learned pages of spells thanks to Abignus. Maybe there was something else she could try. Keeping her eyes closed, she sifted through all of the spells she'd crammed in her head and then she snapped upright.

"I've got it!" she shouted, scrambling to her feet.

"What did you find?" Hugo asked, leaving the helm to join her.

"A spell to put that slimy serpent under my command. If I can control him, I can make him go back to his underwater prison."

"Let me see it." Calla bent to lift the spellbook but Abigail put her hand out, stopping her.

"It's not in the spellbook. It's a possession spell from Madame Arisa's class."

Calla's eyes widened. "That's an advanced spell—and dangerous. We weren't meant to use it. You realize you'd have to actually become Jormungand."

"So?"

"So it sounds dangerous."

"So is a monstrous sea snake loose on the world. I say we try it and see if it works."

"You want to possess me? No thanks," Calla said.

"I'll do it," Hugo volunteered.

Abigail looked at him. "Are you sure? I don't know what will happen."

"I trust you."

"Okay, let's give it a try." Abigail rubbed her suddenly clammy hands down the front of her dress. "Are you ready?"

He nodded, then closed his eyes tight.

"Here goes nothing. *Tempera similus. Tempera morpheus. Tempera transfera.*"

The moment she began speaking the words, Abigail's pulse skyrocketed as if she had run a race. Her hands tingled with power, and her body felt charged with energy. She took two steps back, then ran forward and dove straight at Hugo. There was a moment of friction, and she feared it wasn't going to work. Then it passed, and it was as if Abigail disappeared and reappeared inside Hugo's skin.

She stretched her fingers out, feeling Hugo's fingers move. It was odd to see Hugo's hand through his eyes.

This feels funny, Hugo thought.

How strange! She could hear his thoughts as if he were speaking them out loud. It was a mixed jumble. He was frightened they were going to fail. Worried he was missing schoolwork. Missing his parents. And something else he was hiding. . .

Stop reading my thoughts, he said.

Sorry, I can't help it.

She felt Hugo trying to intrude on her thoughts, but she pushed back, blocking him, and found herself ejected. She flopped back onto the deck. Her legs were rubbery, but triumph raced through her.

"It worked!"

"Yeah." Hugo blinked his eyes. "It was weird when you raised my hand, like I wasn't in control of it. It felt like a spider crawling around my thoughts."

"Could you see mine?" she asked idly.

"Not really. It was like a dark curtain was pulled over them, and I couldn't see behind it."

Relief flooded Abigail. The last thing she needed Hugo to see was the dark paths her thoughts had been taking. "Jasper, how much longer until we reach Fenjoy?"

The old sailor stood on the main sail boom, holding on to the mast and studying the horizon. His shoulders sagged, and he shook his head. "We're too late. Fenjoy's gone."

Agony pierced Abigail's heart. "Too late? No, that's not possible. Keep looking. Maybe we're just off course."

He jumped down onto the deck next to her and put a hand on her shoulder. "I'm a son of Aegir. I never get off course in the seas. I'm telling you, it's gone. A sweep of that serpent's tail is powerful enough to cause an earthquake underwater, break apart the very foundation of an island this size."

"Gone?" A chasm opened up inside Abigail. "It's my fault. If I hadn't waited . . . If I hadn't stayed and done my homework, we might have gotten here in time."

"Abigail, stop," Hugo said. "Capricorn is the one to blame, not you."

She steeled herself not to scream at him that he was wrong, and instead turned back to Jasper. "We have to get to Asgard. Now. Take us there."

Before the old sailor could answer, a mermaid broke the surface, followed by several others. They each held a trident with wicked sharp tines.

"Jasper, son of Aegir," a silver-haired mermaid called out. "The queen of the seas asks for your favor."

Jasper paled, turning on the deck to face them. "What is it she asks?"

"That you come with us to Zequaria, where you will be detained."

"That is her favor?" he asked. "That I come with you?"

The mermaid nodded.

"Agreed."

"Jasper, wait!" Abigail said. "We can't go to Zequaria."

He grabbed her shoulders, pulling her in to whisper in her ear. "We're not. Just me. She wasn't careful with her words."

"But we can't sail the ship without you."

"Hugo knows this ship topside to bottom. Be sure not to take on too much water, and sail north until you find Asgard."

He went to the railing and stood on the side.

"Tell the others to join you," the mermaid said.

"That wasn't part of the deal. The favor was for me to go with you. I'm afraid if you renegotiate, the favor will be canceled."

The mermaid's face turned red. "You know I meant for all of you to come."

"But it is not the agreement we made."

Her eyes narrowed with rage. "Fine. We'll take a son of Aegir. Capricorn will be pleased. Sink the ship," she said to the other mermaids. She pointed her trident at Jasper. Jagged lightning shot out, and wrist cuffs made of light appeared around his wrists. He jumped into the water, disappearing below the surface.

"Quick, we need to get out of here," Abigail said. "Hugo, man the sails. Calla, steer."

The mermaids surrounded the ship. They began attacking it, thrusting with their tridents and battering the wood. Abigail calmly flung witchfire at every mermaid she saw. A pair of them squealed as their hair caught fire. The ship began moving, skimming over the surface.

"Some wind now," she called to Hugo.

They stood behind the sails. He took his medallion, holding it in front of him, and together they cried, "*Ventimus!*" A large gust of wind billowed the sails, and the ship picked up speed, moving swiftly over the water. Abigail went to the railing. The mermaids were falling back. She and Hugo added more wind until they were certain they were out of reach.

Besides a few holes in the sides, the ship was intact.

"What about Jasper?" Hugo said. "We have to rescue him."

"Jasper will be fine," Abigail said. "We have to find Jormungand. The mermaids gave me an idea. Calla, how do you feel about searching for us?"

"Me?"

"Yes. You're part mermaid."

"But I don't even know how to swim," she blurted out.

"Then it's as good a time as any to learn." Abigail gave her a little push her toward the railing.

Hugo stepped in front of them, blocking their path. "Only if Calla wants to."

Abigail glared at him. "Do you want that serpent to destroy another island? I need to find him."

"But only if Calla is willing," he repeated. "Calla, if you don't want to do it, we'll find another way."

The witchling looked terrified as she eyed the dark, rolling waves beneath the ship. "No, it's okay. I'm just scared."

"I'll go with you," Abigail said, her voice gentling.

She took her boots off and shed her dress, going down to the stockings and tank she wore underneath. Calla did the same. They shivered slightly in the breeze. Abigail stepped up onto the railing and held her hand out. Calla joined her. They wavered a moment, and then Abigail jumped, pulling Calla into the water with her. They hit with a loud splash.

Calla floundered, her arms slapping at the surface. Abigail tried to help her, but Calla grabbed on to Abigail's neck, and the two sank. Hugo had clambered over the railing, prepared to jump in, when Abigail surfaced, holding Calla at arm's length.

"Don't fight it," she said, sputtering water out. "Let it come naturally."

"I feel funny," Calla said, her voice high-pitched.

"It's the mermaid in you. Let yourself relax."

Calla calmed, her arms sliding back and forth on the surface to stay afloat. "My legs are itching. I can feel something. Oh!" A ridge of skin rippled along her arm, and then she tipped onto her back as her legs flipped up—only they weren't her legs anymore. They had fused together into a long fin that sparkled with pale pink and green scales.

"This is amazing!" She laughed and swam backward, splashing Hugo in the face with her flipper.

He laughed too. "You're getting the hang of it!"

"I never knew." She dove out of sight while Abigail floated and Hugo watched. She was gone for a good three or four minutes before she shot up to the surface, flinging the water out of her hair as she grinned at them.

"I can breathe underwater. It's fantastic! I really am a mermaid!"

"And a witch," Abigail reminded her. "But right now, we need that mermaid side. Can you lead us to Jormungand?"

She wrinkled her nose. "I don't know how."

"Let yourself feel the sea. I know you can do it. He's a giant serpent—when he swims, he's going to have to give off vibrations. Feel for him."

"All right. I'm going to swim some more. Give me a minute."

Hugo stuck his hand out and hauled Abigail onto the deck, and they waited. They could see a dim outline of the witchling swimming in a circle around their boat, her head going from side to side.

When she finally surfaced, she looked excited. "I'm not sure, but I think he's that way." She pointed toward the north.

"Then that's the way we'll go," Hugo said. "Lead on, and we'll follow." He tossed her a long rope. "Just in case. We don't want to lose you."

She did a somersault and swam off until the rope grew taut. Hugo adjusted the sails, and they began heading north.

"Do you think she knows what she's doing?" Abigail asked.

"Do any of us?"

She sighed. "I suppose not."

"I know you're doing everything you can," he said. "I know you think you have to keep it all inside, but I'm your friend."

"I know."

"And friends don't keep secrets from each other."

"You have a secret."

His jaw dropped, and she held up a hand. "It's okay. I didn't see what it was. But I could tell when I was in your thoughts. You have one."

"I'll tell you mine if you tell me yours." He waited, but she said nothing.

She couldn't tell Hugo about Abignus. He would make her destroy the spellbook, if only to protect her. But Abigail was no longer certain she could do it.

Chapter 18

They sailed on until Calla surfaced, putting her hand up to call a halt.

"Did you find him?" Abigail asked.

Calla nodded, her eyes large in her face. Hugo reached a hand over and pulled her on board. As the air hit her legs, the webbing faded, and they returned to normal. She quickly slipped her dress over her head.

"Where is he?" Hugo asked.

Before Calla could answer, the water swelled, shifting the boat sideways. The tip of the serpent's tail whipped up and then slapped down next to the boat, narrowly missing it.

"We're being attacked!" Hugo shouted.

"We need to move," Abigail said. "Calla, wind spell, now."

She planted her feet on the deck as Calla joined her, and together they thrust their hands in the air, crying, "*Ventimus*!" A sharp gust of wind puffed out the sails, and the ship lurched forward.

Up ahead, the undulating body of the serpent broke the surface. The emerald-green scales shone in the water, and his wedge-shaped head was aimed straight at them.

Abigail could make out a thick collar of seaweed wrapped around his neck, and a familiar woman with flowing green hair stood on top of his head, her feet planted wide as she guided the serpent toward them.

"Capricorn has seen us," Hugo shouted. "We need more than just wind."

Abigail tried to think of a way out, but the serpent was bearing down on them so fast. All she could see were his fangs and angry eyes. Capricorn appeared to be laughing, her face lit up in triumph.

"Think, Abigail, think." Her mind raced through every spell she'd learned but she came up empty. Nothing short of a miracle would save them from the jaws of that oncoming beast.

Let me help, Abignus whispered.

Abigail didn't bother to argue. "Tell me."

Levantus.

"Just one word?"

It's all you need. If you open yourself up to your darkness.

Abigail took in a deep breath, closing her eyes to block out the sight of Capricorn speeding toward them.

"Abigail, do something!" Hugo shouted.

Cold spread through her, reaching her fingertips. When she was ready, she opened her eyes and shouted, "*Levantus!*"

The serpent's maw yawned wide as he leaped from the water, aiming his jaws at them. The head was large enough to swallow three of Jasper's ships whole. But his jaws snapped on empty air as the ship shot up out of the water and out of reach.

Below them, Capricorn let out a squeal of rage as she urged Jormungand around for another pass. The ship was floating over the water, carried forward by the wind. It was taking everything Abigail had to keep it aloft.

Calla leaned over the side, sending down blasts of witchfire until Jormungand suddenly dove, disappearing from sight.

"Do you think they're gone?" she asked.

"No. They're preparing for another strike," Abigail said with certainty. "We need to go higher. Calla, I need your help."

Calla looked frightened. "But I don't have dark magic."

"Yes, you do. All witches have it. You just have to open yourself up to it."

She hesitated.

"Do you want to live or not?" Abigail could feel her strength fading.

"Live," Calla said. She took up a stance next to Abigail. "What do I do?"

"You know that part where your magic comes from, somewhere in the center of you?"

Calla nodded.

"Better hurry," Hugo shouted. "I see movement in the water."

"Tap into that, and then go deeper. Go to where it gets cold and . . . kind of scary."

"I'm not sure what you mean . . . Oh, I see." Her eyes widened. "I didn't know that was there."

"Now, open it wider. Free it into your magic. Then say the word with me. Are you ready?"

"Abigail, he's coming!" Hugo screamed.

"Ready," Calla answered.

They said the spell together. "*Levantus!*"

The ship shot up higher at the same moment the serpent broke the surface. His fangs latched on to the rudder, and they were thrown sideways against the railing. There was a splintering sound, and then the ship broke free,

floating out of reach. A strong gust of wind carried it swiftly forward.

Hugo ran to the side of the ship. "They're leaving!" He turned to grin at them. "Capricorn's giving up."

Abigail slowly released her hold on the ship, letting it drift lower and lower until it settled in the water.

Hugo let out a cheer but Abigail was too shattered to be relieved at their near escape. "She's not giving up, Hugo. She's heading to Asgard. You better go below, see what damage was done."

He nodded and opened the hatch, slipping below deck.

Abigail turned to Calla. The girl had gone completely silent, her hands hanging limp at her side. "Are you all right?"

"Is it always like that?" she asked in a shaky voice.

"Terrifying?"

Calla nodded.

"Yes. But you get used to it." Abigail's knees were like jelly, and she slid down onto the deck, her legs splayed before her. Calla slid down next to her and wrapped her hands around her knees.

"I understand now," Calla said softly. "Why you say you have no choice. It's strange—I quite liked how it felt even though I was frightened."

Hugo popped his head up. "There's a small hole, which I patched, and the rudder is gone, but at least we're not sinking." He hurried over to test out the wheel, but it spun uselessly in his hands. "We'll have to use the sails to steer our course, which is what, by the way?"

"Asgard," Abigail said, fighting back a yawn. Her bones felt leaden, as if every ounce of energy had been leached from her. "We have to follow Capricorn and stop her."

"How do we find it? You heard Jasper—it's never in the same place."

"We head in the same direction as Capricorn and hope for the best."

Abigail's eyelids drooped. A heavy dragging on her made her want to sleep—the price of using that much magic. It took its toll each time. Curling up on her side, she gave up the fight to keep her eyes open and was pulled down into a pit of darkness.

Chapter 19

Abigail was awoken by a splash of water on her cheek. Her eyes flew open and a sense of relief settled over her as her dreams faded away. They had been filled with the gnashing teeth of the serpent and its glowing yellow eyes. She shivered at the sudden drop in temperature as another raindrop splotched on the deck next to her.

Hugo and Calla had their hands on the boom and were pushing it across the ship, moving the position of the sails. The ship tilted as the wind filled out the sails. This was how Hugo was steering; using the wind to push them diagonally, and then back the other way, in hopes of following Capricorn.

"It looks like a storm is moving in," Hugo said grimly. "I'll need you to help Calla while I go down and bail. We're taking on a lot of water."

Abigail stood, craning her neck back. The sky had turned black, as if it were night. Rain began falling in earnest. Her clothes were soon plastered to her skin, and her teeth chattered endlessly as they pushed the boom across the ship every few minutes.

Lightning forked down, hitting the water next to them. The ship dipped in a deep trough, and there was a tearing sound as the main sail split down the center. Waves crashed over the top of the railing, nearly washing Abigail overboard.

Calla grasped her hand and pulled her back to safety. The ship steadied, and then a large wave appeared in front of them, cresting high over the bow. Hugo had just enough time to shout "Hang on" before they were swamped.

The entire boat went underwater. Abigail clung to the mast, but her arms were ripped loose as the water tossed them about. She hit the side of the railing, bruising her ribs. She tried vainly to grab on, but her fingers slipped, and then she was in the sea.

Waves rolled over her, pushing her under. She couldn't breathe or make heads or tails out of which way was up

or down. Her arms flailed, and suddenly her head broke free, and she dragged in a breath. She spun around, trying to see where the ship was, but the waves were too high.

"Hugo! Calla!"

The wind howled, and water sprayed in her face. She could hear that voice in her head screaming at her for being so careless, but she ignored it. "They'll come for me."

They left you, Abignus accused.

"No, they'll circle back. They won't leave me." She searched desperately in every direction and then gave a shout of joy as lightning struck, lighting up the little ship. She could see Calla and Hugo on deck, but they were sailing away from her.

"Here! I'm here!" She shouted until her voice was hoarse.

I told you they couldn't be trusted.

"Stop it!" Tears ran down Abigail's cheeks. "They can't see me, that's all."

She started swimming, trying to catch up to the boat, but the winds were against her, and the boat quickly drifted out of sight. She swam until her arms ached and her teeth chattered so hard she thought they might break. Even her legs were going numb, and part of her wanted to give up. It would be so much easier if she just gave in to the dragging feeling that made her want to stop swimming.

No, we have to live so we can end those wretched friends of yours.

"Oh, b-be quiet," Abigail said. "Unless y-y-you have something u-u-useful to say, like how t-t-t-to get out of here."

For once Abignus went silent, but instead of being relieved, Abigail felt lonelier than ever.

She swam on, hoping against hope the ship would reappear. The seas gradually calmed, and the clouds parted, giving way to weak sunlight. Abigail rolled onto her back and tried to think of a plan. She was lost in the middle of the sea with no sign of land nearby.

Something bumped her arm, and she screamed, fearing it was an akkar, but it was just a piece of driftwood. She turned in the water and gasped. Was that an island? It was small, but it was definitely a land mass. Maybe Hugo and Calla were there waiting. Energized, she started swimming, letting the current tug her closer.

She kept her eyes on the island, afraid it would disappear if she looked away. There wasn't much—just a spit of land in the sea with a jagged peak rising up in the center. A white sandy beach between rocks beckoned her, and she headed for it, letting the waves carry her to shore.

Exhausted, she hauled herself out of the water. Taking her boots off, she dumped the water out and gave her clothes a good wringing before she looked around.

The place looked deserted. No footsteps marred the crystal-white sands. A gurgling noise led her to clamber through the bushes that lined the shore. A bubbling stream ran through some rocks to a small pool. Bending down, she cupped water into her mouth, cautiously tasting it before gulping down handfuls. After the drink she felt better and decided to explore. Hugo and Calla could be on the other side of the island searching for her.

She stuck to the shoreline, avoiding the craggy rocks that formed the island's peak. She called out to Hugo, but the crashing waves blotted out her voice. In less than an hour, she found herself back at her starting point, her tracks clearly visible in the sand.

Sinking down, she wrapped her hands around her knees. Her clothes were growing stiff with salt. The sun was just beginning to dip under the horizon, and her stomach growled with hunger. She'd used a lot of magic lifting the ship; being dumped into the ocean and forced to swim had drained her. But there was no time to sleep. She would have to find shelter and a way off this island. She eyed the peak. Maybe if she climbed to the top, she could see Jasper's sails. She could light a fire and send a signal.

If nothing else, a fire would keep her warm. Abigail turned away from the water and pushed her way through the bushes into the interior of the island. Besides a few scraggly pines and patchy tall grass, nothing much grew here. It felt like an abandoned volcano that had spit up its last bit of lava. Climbing boulder to boulder, she slowly made her way up until she stood on a flat boulder at the highest point. The sun was almost gone, but she took a quick scan in every direction.

Jasper's ship was nowhere to be seen.

She shivered, wondering if she was going to be stuck here forever.

Fire, she told herself. *Start a fire and you'll be rescued.*

Just below the vantage point was a small stand of trees in a circle of boulders. She climbed down and searched for any fallen branches, but the area was clear, as though it had been swept clean. Not even a twig littered the ground. The trees were thin limbed with long silvery leaves and knotted trunks. Thinking it odd that not one leaf had fallen to the ground, Abigail reached up to break off a limb.

"Ouch!" a voice snapped.

The branch whacked Abigail in the face, sending her sprawling backward.

Before she could muster her wits, the three trees shuffled forward as if their roots weren't planted in the ground.

Abigail drew a ball of witchfire, scrambling to her feet. "Stay back. I don't want to have to set fire to you."

Branches knocked together as angry hisses split the air.

"How dare she!"

"Does she not know who we are?"

"The nerve!"

"Who are you?" Abigail asked, keeping the witchfire in front of her.

"You are the intruder," a voice rasped, and the largest of the three trees rattled its branches at her like sabers. "Who are you?"

"I'm Abigail. Abigail Tarkana."

The trees were silent.

"I told you who I am. Now tell me who you are," she demanded, inching closer. Tilting her head, she could just make out faces in the tree trunks. Those knots were a pair of eyes that blinked at her. Peeling bark formed a mouth.

"You should not be here," the tree said. "It is not the right time."

"I fell overboard, and my friends couldn't turn around and get me. Please, do you know how I can get off this island? There's something that I have to do. If I don't, terrible things will happen."

"Turn around," one of them said. "Don't look at us."

Abigail hesitated.

"We won't harm you," the tree chided.

She turned her back on them and let her witchfire die out. She listened hard, hearing the rustle of leaves and rasp of bark.

"You may turn around," the voice said, only this time it didn't sound quite so raspy.

When she turned, three women stood in place of the trees. They each wore a simple gown of gauzy material. Silvery hair fell to their waists, braided with leaves and twigs. The only difference between them was their ages—as if they were the same person at different times. One was young, barely out of her teens; the other, middle-aged; and the last, elderly.

"Nice to meet you, Abigail Tarkana. We are the Norns," the oldest one said. "I am Urd, goddess of the past."

The middle-aged one said, "And I am Verdoni, goddess of the present."

The youngest waved her hand and said shyly, "I am Skald, goddess of the future."

"You're the Norns? But don't they decide the fates?" Abigail tried to remember what she'd learned in her History of Witchery class.

"We don't decide the fates—we help shape them as events unfold," Verdoni said. "Hence you are here today and not tomorrow or yesterday."

"But . . . you said I shouldn't be here."

She shrugged. "It is a sign of what you are becoming."

"What do you mean?"

"What is to be is being written," the youngest one, Skald, said cryptically. "It's right there on our loom."

Verdoni waved a graceful arm behind her. In the shelter of the rocks stood three golden looms racked with shining white thread. Bolts of fabric were stacked next to each loom.

"I weave what *can* be," Skald said. "The hope for the future."

"I weave what *is* becoming," Verdoni said. "The present."

"And I weave what has already happened," Urd said. "If you have found yourself here, your fate is at a crossroad. A choice must be made."

"I don't understand."

"Don't you, dark witch?" Urd moved closer, walking around Abigail as if inspecting her. "You are meant to be the Curse Breaker, the one who would free the witches from Odin's control, but instead you fall deeper under the spell of darkness."

"I don't mean to." Abigail twisted her hands, her heart thumping in her chest.

"I think you do. I think that is your fate," Urd said.

"No! There has to be another way."

"When you have to choose, you always choose the easy path," Verdoni said, turning to retrieve a long stretch of fabric. "Here and here, everywhere I see you let your emotions tug you, never stopping to think of the cost."

"I think of the cost. It's just . . . I never have a choice. I can't just let my friends suffer. I have to do something."

"You cast three helpless witchlings into the netherworld, and a part of you was happy," Verdoni said.

"I rescued them," Abigail said defensively. "I didn't mean for it to happen."

"You let Odin's Stone be destroyed and started a war," Urd accused.

"If I hadn't, Robert would have died."

She waved a hand. "One death when so many perished in the war."

"I know . . . but I couldn't do it."

"You used it again today saving yourself from that serpent that your actions unleashed on the world."

Abigail's shoulders sagged. "I told you. I had no choice. My friends' lives were in danger."

Urd smiled, but it was a sad smile. "We don't argue your choices or fault you for them. We observe the path you are on and the choices you make and then predict your fate. Would you like to know the fate we see? The one that you are making?"

Abigail had an overwhelming urge to shake her head, but she had to know. "Yes."

Skald went first. The young Norn held up a piece of fabric. "So much power in you . . . Comes from your father, I suppose. With bloodlines such as yours, it was inevitable you would have two paths to choose from."

"Two paths?" Vor had said the very same thing to her.

"Yes, one of light and one of dark. The light is growing faint. I can barely make out the threads anymore," she said sadly, "while the path of dark grows more and more clear. Your mother faced a similar path but in the end she chose light, even though it cost her her life."

Verdoni went on. "The loom shows me that based on the path you are on, you rise to rule the Tarkana coven, in spite of failing at breaking Odin's curse. Your magic grows in intensity until no other creature in Orkney can match you. Your magic will grow and grow until it consumes you."

"What do you mean consume me?"

She held up a finger. "Darkness swallows light. The things you care about, you will lose."

"Like what?"

"Your friend, the Balfin boy, he will perish first. That will cost you part of your soul."

Dread filled her. "Perish how?"

"It won't matter. You won't be there to save him."

"But—"

The Norn went on. "Your friend, the son of Odin—he too will be lost in your search for power. And another piece of your soul lost will drive you further into the darkness until there is nothing in front of you but the need for revenge, for control, to fight back at what is really only yourself and your own doing."

Tears blinded Abigail's eyes. "I don't want that. Please tell me how to change it."

The Norns put the fabric away. "Verdoni is beginning her weaving. Soon it will be complete, and then there will be no changing it. The path narrows in front of you, and there will be no turning from it."

"But how do I stop Jormungand and Capricorn without using dark magic?"

"Magic itself is not dark," Urd said. "It is the heart of the wielder that twists it into something that taints the soul. The question is, what is in your heart Abigail Tarkana?"

The last bit of sun faded as twilight set in. A breeze blew through, and in the next instant, the women were trees again.

"Can you at least tell me how to get off this island?" Abigail asked.

"Your friends await you down on the shore," the eldest said. "Hurry, or they will believe you to be still at sea."

Abigail backed away as the trees waved their branches in farewell, speaking in unison: "We will meet again, Abigail Tarkana."

Abigail turned and ran as if a Shun Kara wolf were nipping at her heels. She burst through the brush onto the beach, sure that her friends had already sailed away, only to see Jasper's rickety boat tied off to a tree. Two figures sat around a small fire.

Relief coursed through her so sharply her knees sagged.

"Hugo." Her voice croaked as she called to him.

Both Hugo and Calla turned in surprise, and their faces lit up as they hurried to her side.

"Abigail! We've been so worried!" Hugo flung his arms around her, and Calla joined from the other side, forming a tight circle.

"I . . . I thought you left me," Abigail hiccupped between sobs that shook her frame.

"Left you?" Hugo pulled away, his face a mixture of shock and surprise in the firelight. "Why would you ever think that?"

"We've been searching for you for hours," Calla said. "The wind drove us on until the storm abated, and as soon as it did, we turned around and headed straight back. Hugo was clever and fashioned a new rudder and I patched the main sail while we waited."

They guided her to the fire, and they all sat down. Hugo passed her his mug, and she took a sip, grateful for the hot tea.

"I didn't know what to think," Abigail said, wiping the tears away with her sleeve. "I think I was just scared." She debated telling them about the Norns but decided it was better to keep that to herself. "Now that you've found me, we should be leaving. Capricorn could be all the way to Asgard by now."

"We can't leave until the tide comes back in," Hugo said.

"Hugo's right," Calla said, stretching and letting out a big yawn. "I feel like I could sleep for a week." She curled up on her side, pulling her blanket around her and promptly fell asleep.

Hugo passed Abigail a blanket and they lay down on the sand. The stars blazed in the sky—a million twinkling lights.

Abigail searched for her father's star. There. A faint blue light that shone steadily.

"Do you think he's watching you right now?" Hugo asked in the darkness.

Abigail swallowed. "Maybe." *Would he be proud of the witchling she was or ashamed?*

"If he is, he would be so proud," Hugo said, as if he could read her thoughts.

Abigail's heart clenched. "Why do you say that?"

He rolled on his side to study her in the dim light of the embers. "Because you're brave. You do the hard things that I could never do, even when it costs you. And you never give up. You're the strongest person I've ever met."

Abigail listened to her heart beating in her chest. Every beat was like a warning that Hugo was wrong. That he didn't know her at all. That she was the farthest thing from brave.

Chapter 20

Hugo was up with the sun. He looked over at Abigail, relieved to see her sleeping soundly. She had tossed and turned during the night, muttering about talking trees and someone named Abignus in her sleep. Her face had been frantic when she had appeared out of the bushes, as though she had really believed they would just abandon her. Why would she ever think that? Didn't she know she was Hugo's best friend? And friends didn't abandon one another.

Sighing, he stood and started readying the ship. The girls quietly waded out and joined him on deck. The tide had rolled in, and it was easy enough to push the ship off. He quickly set the sails, and the gentle breeze began moving their ship away from the island. Looking back, he frowned. The peak in the center didn't seem so high now. He blinked, and the island looked even lower in the water.

"Is the island sinking?"

Calla and Abigail turned to look at it, gasping as the tip disappeared from sight.

"What happened?" Calla asked. "Did Jormungand do that?"

"I don't know," Abigail said, looking suddenly pale. "But we can't worry about it. We need to find Asgard. Hugo, any ideas?"

Before Hugo could explain he had no idea how to find an island of the gods, something bumped against the side of the boat. He leaned over the edge and spied a long piece of wood floating in the water. More debris bobbed next to it, along with a sleeping pad.

"It looks like a ship went down close by," Hugo said. "I thought I saw a sail when the storm hit, just before Abigail was washed overboard. I'm going to climb the mast and see if I can spot anything. There could be survivors."

Calla gave him a boost. He wrapped his legs around the pole, inched his way to the top, and searched the horizon, using his hand to shade his eyes.

The water was calm enough. There were scattered planks of wood and a large piece of canvas still attached to a mast. The ship couldn't have been that large. The mast wasn't much bigger than Jasper's.

Something pale flopped in the water, like a fish jumping. Or was that a hand rising?

"I see something!" he shouted. "Over there."

Calla quickly turned the ship, guiding it in the direction he pointed. Hugo kept his eyes glued to the spot where he'd seen the movement.

"Here," he called.

Abigail dropped the sail, and the ship slowed to a stop. Hugo quickly climbed down, and they looked over the side.

The surface was calm. There was no sign of whatever he'd seen.

"Maybe it was a fish," Calla said.

"I don't think so." Certainty gripped him, giving him a sudden burst of courage. Stepping up on the railing, Hugo took his glasses off and dove in. He split the surface and went deeper, searching in every direction.

There. Something was slowly sinking below him.

Next to him, Calla hit the water, quickly changing into a mermaid. She darted ahead of Hugo down to the floating figure and hauled him upward.

Shock made Hugo choke underwater as he recognized the blurry face.

It was Robert Barconian.

Hooking their arms under his, they swiftly made it back to the surface with Calla's powerful fins.

"Abigail, some help," Hugo called.

She leaned over and grabbed Robert's shoulders, holding him above water until Hugo climbed out. Together they pulled him in, then helped Calla up to the railing.

"Is he breathing?" Calla asked.

Abigail put her ear to his chest. "It's not rising."

Hugo put his hands on Robert's chest and began pressing up and down. "I saw Jasper do this once to a sailor who fell overboard." On the third press, Robert's stomach heaved, and then he spit out a lungful of water on the deck, coughing and gasping.

When he opened his eyes, he looked shocked to see the three of them.

"Abigail! Hugo! And Calla too! How did you find me?"

"Hugo saw your sails just before the storm hit," Abigail said. "What are you doing out here?"

His face darkened. "It was that mermaid queen. I thought she was on our side, but she's released a monstrous serpent."

"We know. That's why we're here. How did you end up out here?"

"My father wanted to go to Asgard and plead with Odin to help us stop Jormungand, but he couldn't leave

Garamond unprotected. I told him I would go in his place, but he refused."

"So you stole a ship," Abigail guessed, rolling her eyes.

He nodded. "There was a terrible storm like nothing I've ever seen. The ship was struck by lightning. Put a hole in the deck right through the bottom."

"Well, it's a good thing we came along," Hugo said. "Any idea how to find Asgard?"

Robert pulled off the leather satchel still strapped across his chest. Dumping the water out, he took out a large brass compass that fit in both his hands. The face was lined with runic symbols.

"This belongs to my father. This symbol here"—he pointed at an upside-down fork—"is the symbol for Asgard." He shook it, but the needle moved listlessly in whatever direction he tilted it.

"It looks broken," Calla said.

Robert sagged. "I know. I've been sailing in circles for days."

Hugo took it from him, turning it over in his hands. "Maybe you just need to try something new." He went to the helm and set it on the wooden stand.

"Like what?" Robert asked. "I've shaken it. Held it up to the sky. I nearly tossed it overboard."

"Maybe you just have to ask it to take you where you want to go," Hugo said calmly.

Robert gaped at him. "You want me to talk to a compass?"

Hugo shrugged. "Do you have a better idea?"

Robert was silent and then he shook his head. "No." He put his hands on the wheel. "I'll try anything. Tell me what to do."

"Think of Asgard. Think of your father. Think about what it means to be a son of Odin."

"You mean the son who destroyed Odin's Stone?" Robert choked out, but he gripped the wheel tighter and cleared his throat. "Okay, here goes nothing. I'd like to go to Asgard."

They all peered over his shoulder at the compass.

The needle wavered and then sagged toward the bottom. He tapped the glass. "Compass, I command you to show me the way to Asgard."

The needle spun in a circle and then drooped to the bottom again.

"Maybe some magic?" Hugo suggested.

Calla and Abigail put their hands on the brass casing.

"I can feel its power," Abigail said. "Perhaps some witchfire will start it up."

She and Calla each drew a small ball of witchfire and pressed them against the compass, but the magic snuffed out in their hands.

"It's no use," Abigail began, when suddenly the needle flickered.

"Did you see that?" Robert asked.

"Yes. It moved!" Hugo said. "Look, it's spinning in a circle."

Calla looked worried. "Do you think we broke it?"

"No, I think it's searching for Asgard," Robert turned the compass from side to side until the needle pegged on the upside-down fork.

"That's it!" He set the compass back on the helm and gave the wheel a hard wrench. "Hugo, man the sails. We have our course."

"Do you think we'll get there before Capricorn?" Abigail asked.

"Odin's island cannot be found unless he wills it to be," Robert said confidently. "I'm sure that sea witch is still drifting around the seas searching."

Hugo did his best to handle the sails, but the seas grew rougher as the day wore on. Abigail moved to stand in the front of the boat, her arms wrapped around her middle to protect her from the wind. At times she seemed to be talking to herself, almost as if she were arguing with herself. It was so strange, Hugo wanted to confront her, but he was too busy trying to keep the ship from capsizing in the heavy winds.

Robert held on grimly to the wheel, unwilling to let go lest the compass change its mind.

"We need to drop the sails," Hugo said as a fresh gust of wind tipped the boat on its side. "It looks like another storm's coming in."

"No. We keep going," Robert said stubbornly.

Calla came up from the galley with two steaming mugs of stew. She shoved one in Hugo's hand, and held out the other to Robert. "Let me take the wheel."

He hesitated.

"You've been at it all day. Eat, and then you can have it back," she said.

He nodded, sinking down on a cushion and gratefully cradled the mug, shoveling the food in as fast as he could.

"What's with Abigail?" He nodded at her stiff figure. "She's been up there for hours."

Calla kept her hands steady on the wheel. "Abigail is going through something. When she's ready to tell us, she will. Do you think we're getting close?"

Robert scraped the remains of the stew into his mouth before swiping his arm across his chin. "Who knows? My father said the compass wasn't a guarantee of finding Asgard. Odin has to want you to find it."

"How did he come to have the compass?" Hugo asked.

"It's one of the few tokens Odin gifted us with, like Odin's Stone. It's only to be used in dire times. My father will never forgive me if I lose it."

"It doesn't get much more dire than an angry mermaid queen with a monstrous serpent that can destroy the world at her command, now does it?" Hugo pointed out. "Besides, if we succeed, he'll be so busy praising you as a hero he won't notice a missing compass."

Robert thought it over. "And if we don't?"

"Then it won't much matter will it?"

Chapter 21

Abigail ignored the knifing cold, her arms clutched around her middle as she battled the feelings inside her. Guilt was tearing her apart. Guilt over what was happening. Guilt over using dark magic and liking it. Guilt over not being able to throw the cursed spellbook away.

Stop fighting what is only your true nature.

Like a cat rousing from sleep, the darkness in her uncoiled.

The Norns were wrong, you know. There is only one path before you.

Not wanting the others to notice she was talking to herself, Abigail turned her face toward the sea. "I thought you were gone," she said quietly, not minding the stinging spray.

Where would I go? I am you.

"Where is Vertulious?"

That old goat sleeps all the time. He really is no use.

"What use are you?"

Did you not hear the Norns? Our magic is going to make us the most powerful witch that ever lived.

"At what price?" Abigail whispered, turning to look at her friends over her shoulder. "I won't lose them just to become the most powerful witch in the coven."

Who said you had a choice?

There was a mocking laugh, and Abigail seethed, feeling helpless to escape it. "I hate you."

Yet even as you claim to hate me, you won't give our magic up, will you, dark witch? So what does that really make us?

Abigail was about to argue when she spied something rising from the sea. "There!" She raised her arm, pointing. "I see something."

The others rushed to the side of the boat. An island was barely visible, jutting up from a cloak of fog.

"That must be it," Robert said. He checked the compass; the needle pointed straight ahead. "Prepare for landing."

Hugo got the lines ready, standing up front next to Abigail. "Can you believe it? The home of Odin."

A thrill of excitement ran through her, wiping away the darkness that Abignus always visited on her. "The good news is there's no sign of Capricorn."

The hull scraped bottom, and Hugo jumped into knee-deep water, pulling the boat as high as he could and tying the rope to a large boulder.

The fog was so thick they could barely see more than a few feet. The sand stretched out in both directions. When they headed inland, they were met with a thick barrier of shrubbery.

"This brush is impossible," Calla said, tugging uselessly on the branches.

"Odin's refuge can only be accessed by a descendant of his," Hugo said. "So maybe Robert needs to go first."

"Good thing we fished you out of the water," Abigail said. "Go ahead, lead the way."

"Er, I'm not sure how it works." He put a hand on the thick foliage, pushing it aside. It gave way under his hands, creating an opening. He stepped through, disappearing inside. The foliage slowly closed up behind him.

"Hey!" Abigail tried to tug it aside. "Wait for us."

Robert's head poked out, a big grin on his face. "You have to see this."

He widened the opening, propping a stick between the limbs so they could climb through. On the other side, everything was different. The fog dissipated, leaving the sky as blue and bright as anything they had ever seen. The air was warm, almost humid. Abigail ducked as a strange bird with a bright yellow chest streaked past them, peering at her with curious eyes.

"This place is amazing," Hugo said. "I've never seen trees like this."

The trees towered overhead, their branches interlacing and forming a canopy.

"What kind of plants are these?" Calla knelt to put her hand near a purple-and-orange plant with a large round flower.

A sense of danger came over Abigail. "Be careful," she warned as the plant's mouth opened and a yellow pistil shot out, lashing at Calla's hand.

She hissed in pain and jerked back. "Ouch."

"This place isn't what it seems," Robert said. "Odin protects what is his."

They stepped over a narrow stream. Pink fish swam in the shallows, but no one tried to touch them. Calla's hand had a large welt on it that even her healing spell didn't help.

"Where do we find Odin?" Abigail asked. "Does he have a house here?"

Robert shrugged. "All I know is this place is like a refuge to Odin. He comes here to get away from Valhalla and the other gods."

"How big is it?" Calla asked.

"No one knows. There's no map. I overheard my father talking to Rego. They were planning on searching for the Yggdrasil tree—the tree of life that connects his realms. There's a squirrel there named Ratatosk. He can speak—he might know where to find Odin."

"Then we look for a talking squirrel," Abigail said.

Chapter 22

*e*ndera clung to the railing, her stomach turning over and over until her breakfast spilled out over the side. Next to her, Glorian and Nelly were suffering in the same way. Damarius wobbled on his feet, his head hanging low. The ship would not stop rolling from side to side, as if the seas were mad at them.

Even the crew was looking green around the gills.

"Maybe we should go home." Nelly's usual sneer had been replaced with a weary look of fear.

"No. We can't go back," Endera said, even as her hands trembled and another wave of nausea overtook her.

"Witchling." The captain tapped her on the shoulder. He was younger than the other captain and had been mostly cooperative, but he looked grim. "We are nearly out of supplies. We were only supposed to be gone a few days. We cannot keep this up."

"We are not turning around." Endera whirled away to stare out into the gray fog. "It has to be here."

He shook the piece of paper at her, the map she had taken off Solara. "This tells us nothing. It's stopped showing us anything new." He hurled the map into the sea.

Endera watched it slowly sink, along with her hopes of returning triumphant. He spoke the truth. At first, Endera had been so certain they would be there in no time. The familiar islands of the realm had been scratched in rust-colored ink—the blood of a descendant of Odin, if Solara were to be believed. And then a new island had appeared, pulsing on the paper with a faint glow. They had made haste toward it but found nothing, and the glowing island had faded away.

"Threaten me with witchfire if you must but I can't have the men starving or risk mutiny." He strode back to his helm leaving Endera to stare into the gray fog as if she could will Odin's cursed island into existence.

"I'm ready to get off this ship," Glorian said. "Solid ground never sounded better."

Another wave lifted the ship up, and Endera braced for the swoop down that would tip her stomach again, but as the ship breached the top of the wave, something loomed in the gray fog.

"Wait, I see something," she shouted, pointing.

The captain rushed to the side, holding a thin telescope, and searched. "Where?"

"It was right there." She frantically scanned the dense fog.

"I'm sorry, I don't see it," he said. "We turn around."

"No. We're close," Endera pleaded.

"Witchling, it's over. We're turning around before it's too late and we die out here."

He was right. But Endera refused to give up. Not when she was this close. "Fine. Turn around. Leave us here."

"What?" Glorian and Nelly said in unison.

"What do you mean leave us here?" Glorian's lips trembled.

"I'm not swimming in that," Nelly said. "We'll drown for sure."

"We're not going to swim," Endera snapped. "The captain will give us the rowboat."

He scratched at the three-day growth of hair on his chin. "A small boat like that will swamp in these swells. I can't do that."

Endera drew her shoulders back. "I wasn't asking permission. Either you stay and help us search, or you leave us to do it." Inside she was trembling, but there was no way she could turn back. Madame Hestera would never forgive her for stealing the scroll and failing in the mission. "Nelly, gather our things from our cabin while the captain readies the boat for us."

"I never met a more stubborn witchling," he muttered but nodded to one of his men, who began to undo the ropes that lashed the small rowboat to the rigging of the ship.

As the boat splashed down onto the water, a wave nearly swamped it. The captain tossed a bucket in as Nelly rejoined them with a single satchel in her hands, Glorian trailing behind her. She shoved it at Endera.

"Sorry, Endera. You're a good friend and all, but I can't do this."

"You're not coming with me?" Endera asked, shocked.

"No."

"Coward," Endera hissed, turning to Glorian. "I guess it's just you and me then."

But Glorian took a hasty step back toward Nelly. "Sorry, Endera, I can't swim that well. If the boat sinks, that's it for me."

Endera gaped at her two friends and then felt the shock harden into bitterness. "Fine. I don't need you."

Turning on her heel, she climbed over the railing and let the captain lower her into the boat. She held herself rigid, refusing to give into the icy fear that gripped her insides. Before she could tell him no, Damarius leaped over the railing and landed at her feet in the center of the boat. Waves sloshed over the edge, and the water went up to her ankles. She bailed some water out and then gripped the oars, nodding at the captain to toss the rope in.

As the rope hit the boat, the waves swept her away from the safety of the ship. She tugged on the oars, refusing to look at the faces of her friends as they drifted farther and farther away.

Endera kept rowing, fighting the waves, trying to keep the boat from swamping. Her arms ached, and her palms quickly blistered. Water filled the small boat, and she had to pause between rows to bail it out. After an endless hour had passed with no sign of land, she let out a scream of frustration. It was impossible. She should have stayed on the ship and taken whatever punishment Madame Hestera meted out to her. She missed Glorian and Nelly. She had never been alone like this before.

Damarius nosed his head onto her lap, and she buried her face in his fur, sobbing. She was so lost in her misery she didn't notice that the waters had calmed and the little boat had stopped rocking about. It wasn't until it bumped into something solid that she raised her head, gasping in shock. She had run into an island. Somehow her little boat had found dry ground. Not caring whether it was Asgard or the moon, she steered the boat around the outcrop of rock, searching for a sandy beach to land on. She couldn't make out much of the interior because it was shrouded with fog.

Spying a sliver of sand, she rowed the boat over, jumped onto dry ground, and tugged the boat a safe distance onto shore before collapsing on the beach. Damarius jumped out and ran in circles around her, as happy as she was to be on solid ground. The narrow beach was bounded by rocks on either end. Thick foliage hemmed it in.

She strapped her satchel across her shoulders and checked to make sure the scroll was safely tucked inside. Satisfied, she pushed on the nearest shrub, trying to part the branches, but whenever she did, another branch appeared to block her way. Flustered, she called up a ball of witchfire and threw it at the mass of branches, but the fire just sputtered out, and the branches remained unchanged.

"Fine," she said, eyeing the boulders that blocked the sand. "Have it your way." She began climbing the boulder, hoping there was another way to the interior of the island. When she reached the top, she discovered another beach on the other side just like the first.

Dropping onto the sand, she hurried to the thick green shrubs and was unsurprised to find them just as dense and impossible to pass through as the first. Frustrated, she slumped down into the sand. Why must everything be so difficult? And then she heard voices.

Was that Abigail?

Damarius growled low in his throat. Shushing him, she crept to a bend in the shrubs, peeking around and caught her breath.

Not only was it Abigail, but she had those rotten friends of hers with her. Calla, the Balfin boy, and . . . Her heart skipped a beat. Was that the Barconian boy? What was he doing here? Their rickety ship was tied to a rock, and they were trying to enter the interior. Her eyes widened as

Robert disappeared inside, and then she remembered he was a son of Odin. It must grant him passage. The others followed behind him.

Without hesitating, she raced down the sand to the same spot and dove through, with Damarius on her heels.

Chapter 23

The beauty of Asgard paled after several hours of walking through endless forests that led nowhere. The scenery didn't change, and there was no sign of the magnificent Yggdrasil tree where Odin's talking squirrel might be found.

Robert stopped and kicked a tree trunk. "What if it's this one? How do we know Odin's tree isn't any one of these?"

"I've seen a drawing in one of my textbooks," Hugo said. "It's much taller and more majestic. Certainly bigger than these trees."

"Then where is it?" Robert complained. "We've been walking for hours, and I could eat a small cow right about now."

A twig snapped, and Abigail whirled around. She'd felt eyes on them for a while, as if someone were following them. Maybe one of Odin's emissaries. Maybe even an old friend.

"Fetch?" she called out. "Is that you?" They had met Odin's furry green pest several times. Maybe he could lead them to Odin. "Come on, if it's you, don't be shy. We're tired and hungry."

The forest was silent. Whatever had stepped on the twig wasn't coming out.

"We have to keep walking," Hugo said. "We'll find Odin eventually."

"What if he's not even here?" Calla asked with a frown. "He could be anywhere."

"He has to be here," Abigail said. "We need his help stopping Capricorn. Come on."

Time was slipping away. Every second they delayed was one second Capricorn and her giant sea snake were closer to destroying everything.

The ground rumbled under their feet. "What was that?" Hugo asked.

The earth shook again, and a tree split nearby as if something had knocked it over.

They crept closer, ducking behind some bushes, and peered out. Before them was the strangest sight.

A towering bear three times the height of Abigail and dressed in leather armor rose up on its hind legs. On the bear's head was a helmet of leather and metal, and an eyepatch covered one eye. One of its massive paws held a round wooden shield, while the other carried a broadsword it was using to swipe at a tree branch. Something was moving on the branch, staying just out of reach of the giant blade. Abigail squinted. Was that a squirrel?

"Got you!" the bear roared, swinging the sword in a mighty stroke that took the top of the tree off. The squirrel nimbly jumped through the air and landed on the next tree branch, chittering with laughter.

The bear roared in outrage, but it didn't sound angry. It was almost as if they were playing a game.

Abigail stepped out of the bushes. Robert grabbed her arm, holding her back. "Are you crazy? That bear could take your head off."

"We need help finding Odin. Unless you have a better idea?" Shrugging free, she walked into the clearing. "Hello."

At the sound of her voice, the bear swung around, instantly dropping into a crouch. It held the shield in front of it and the sword ready to attack.

"Who trespasses on my island?" it bellowed, then let out a warning roar.

Abigail held her ground. "It's not your island. It's Odin's. And we're here to warn him and ask for his help."

The squirrel jumped from the tree and landed on the bear's shoulder, running down its burly arm to jump down into the grass. It strutted back and forth as it studied Abigail, its bushy red head cocked to the side.

"You're a witch," it pronounced.

Behind her, the others stepped out, and the bear growled in its throat. "More trespassers?"

"We're together," Abigail said. "We are looking for the Yggdrasil tree. We need to find Odin and warn him something terrible is going to happen."

"You can tell me," the squirrel said, flicking one paw. "I work for His Highest himself."

"You're Ratatosk!" Hugo crouched down. "Nice to meet you. I'm Hugo, and you met Abigail."

The squirrel glared at her then sniffed at Calla. "Another witch?"

"Yes, but they're good witches," Hugo said. "And this is Robert. He's a son of Odin."

The squirrel's eyes widened, and it bowed. "Then it truly is an honor."

Ratatosk extended his arm toward the bear. "This mighty beast is known as . . ." The bear growled a warning, and the squirrel hesitated, then said, "Brunin."

The bear watched them with its single eye but said nothing.

"What message have you for Odin?" Ratatosk asked. "I'm his most trusted advisor."

The bear coughed behind its paw as the squirrel puffed out its chest.

"Capricorn has released Jormungand from his prison," Abigail said.

The bear roared in anger. "You lie!" He slammed his sword into the ground in front of them, spraying them with dirt. "The Midgard Serpent is locked safely away under the sea."

"No," Robert said. "He is free. My father sent me to warn Odin and ask for his help."

"Warn him . . . why?" Brunin growled.

"Capricorn wants to destroy Asgard," Abigail said.

Brunin chuckled, and the squirrel rolled in the grass, chittering hysterically.

"That mermaid queen can't destroy Asgard," Brunin said.

"Maybe not, but she can have Jormungand destroy this island."

The bear's eyes blazed with fury. "She wouldn't dare."

"She already destroyed one," Calla said.

"Which?" the beast demanded in an angry growl.

"Fenjoy."

Brunin's shoulders sagged. "A miserable hunk of rock, but the fishing was nice. What does Capricorn want?"

"She wants Odin to strip Aegir and Ran of their powers and make her goddess of the seas. If he doesn't, she's going to unleash Jormungand on all of Orkney, including this island. We need to find a way to get him back in his cell."

The massive bear seemed lost in thought, and then he shook himself. "I can't help you. You should go."

He nodded at Ratatosk and turned to take his leave.

Abigail formed a ball of witchfire and threw it at the massive bear's backside, making Brunin whirl in outrage to glare at her with his one good eye.

"How dare you," he snarled.

"I dare because you're not listening. I think you know how to find Odin, and we're not leaving until we find him and talk to him."

"It won't do you any good," Brunin growled. "Odin cannot interfere."

"Why not?"

"Because it doesn't suit him." The bear knelt down to bring his face closer to hers. "You look capable."

Abigail sputtered with shock. "M-me? I'm just a secondling."

"You're much more than that." His good eye stared into hers. It held a strange power, as if he could see right through her. Then the bear stood. "It is better you leave this island. It is not safe for you to be here."

Ratatosk ran up the bear's leg and jumped on his shoulder, chattering loudly in squirrel talk. Brunin just growled, but the squirrel didn't give up, gesturing wildly with its small hands until finally the bear grunted. He gave them one last look and then turned to lumber off through the trees.

The squirrel dropped to the ground. "The boss says I can assist you in your search."

"The boss? I thought you said Odin was your boss," Hugo said.

"He's the boss. The highest."

"Then who was that?" Abigail asked.

The squirrel grinned. "The boss."

"That was Odin?" Abigail blinked. No wonder she had felt such power. "Wait. He needs to come back. We need his help." She started after him, but the squirrel hopped in front of her.

"He cannot help you. Not now. Things must unfold as they do."

"But if that was Odin, how come he didn't know about the Midgard Serpent?" Robert asked. "Doesn't he know everything that goes on around here?"

The squirrel shrugged its tiny shoulders. "Yes, but when the boss is here on this island, he is shielded from the outside world. It is the only time he rests."

"So he's just going to sit around and let this place be destroyed?" Abigail asked, shocked at his disregard for a world he claimed to protect.

The squirrel took her hand in its small paws. "No, young Abigail. He trusts you will stop that from happening. Come, we mustn't delay. Time is of the essence."

Chapter 24

Endera trembled with excitement from her hiding spot in the bushes at the edge of the clearing. That cowardly bear was the mighty god Odin? Then so be it. She would deliver her message to this Brunin personally and hope he didn't take her head off with that broadsword of his. At her side, Damarius whined softly, but she shushed him. "Come on, we have to keep that bear in sight."

Leaving the others in the clearing, she circled around, easily following the giant bear's tracks deeper into the woods. The sky grew dimmer as the thick foliage closed in over her head. Damarius kept his nose to the ground, following the bear's scent.

Up ahead, she saw something moving through the trees, and her heart quickened.

"Odin, wait," she called. The figure halted.

Brunin had shrunk in size and was now only slightly larger than a grown man, but he still looked fierce. He waited patiently as she approached. Her heart was in her throat. Her hands were shaking so badly she almost dropped the scroll as she pulled it out of her bag.

"My name is Endera."

"I know who you are," Brunin growled.

"Um. Good. Then you know I'm a witch."

The bear nodded. "Why are you here, Endera Tarkana? Have you not suffered enough loss?"

Her heart tripped. How did he know? "What do you mean?"

Brunin shrugged. "You miss your mother. And you come with the desire to rid the world of me."

"No, I came with a message of warning from Madame Hestera." She thrust the scroll at him, but he didn't take it.

"What does it say?" he asked.

"I don't know. I haven't read it." Her voice caught, and she had the sudden urge to tell the truth. "I wasn't supposed to be the one to bring it. Another witchling was."

"But you wanted the fame."

"Yes. And to prove I could do it."

He nodded at her outstretched hand. "That scroll contains a deadly poison."

She flinched, wanting to drop it, but she girded herself with the truth. "No. Madame Hestera wanted you to know we weren't responsible for Jormungand's release. I heard her myself." She began to unroll it, but he swiped it away with his paw. The scroll hit the ground and unfurled. Inside, the page was blank, and a cloud of green smoke wafted up from it. He blew out a large breath, sending the cloud of poison away.

"What was that?" she asked, trembling inside.

"A poison potent enough to sicken even a god like me." The bear shimmered and then became a human figure, a man with a white beard.

Endera gasped. "Are you really Odin?"

He nodded.

She hesitated. "But I thought he lost an eye to gain wisdom." This being had a pair of bright blue eyes that seemed to see right through her.

Odin waved a hand over his face, and the eye appeared sewn shut. "You're correct. To a scoundrel named Mimir who promised me wisdom in exchange. I can appear as many things in many ways." He put one hand on her shoulder. "Someone has betrayed the witches. Take that message back to Hestera and give her my thanks. I believe she meant to warn me."

And then the god turned into an eagle and took flight through the trees.

Endera stood shaking long after he was gone. She had delivered her warning, only to almost kill Odin. Why hadn't he struck her down on the spot? And if it wasn't Madame Hestera who had sent the poison, who had?

Damarius licked her hand, bringing her back to the present.

"We have to get home. Something is very wrong."

Chapter 25

"Where are we going?" Abigail called out as they hurried after the squirrel. It raced ahead, darting back and forth and up trees, then back down again.

"The boss keeps them here somewhere," it said.

"Keeps what where?"

"The chains you need."

"What chains?" Robert asked.

"The ones Odin used to bind Jormungand," Hugo said excitedly. "You know where Odin's chains are?"

The squirrel stopped, drawing itself up to its full height. "I told you I am Odin's trusted assistant. I know where he keeps everything."

"Then lead on."

The squirrel's nose twitched. "It's just . . . I'm turned around."

"You're lost?" Calla said. "But I thought you lived here."

"I do. But this island is bigger than it appears. I may have taken a wrong turn back at that last tree."

The squirrel raced up a trunk all the way to the top and looked around, hanging off a branch with one hand.

It let out an excited chitter and raced down, leaping the last few feet to land in front of them.

"Told you I knew my way around. It's right over there." It stuck its tiny paw out, pointing.

"The chains?" Hugo asked.

"No. The tree."

The squirrel raced ahead. They hurried after and emerged from the forest into a large clearing. In the center, a magnificent tree towered over their heads, spreading out in a broad canopy.

"Is that the Yggdrasil tree?" Hugo asked, craning his head back in awe.

"I'm more worried about that snake." Robert pointed at the trunk.

A thick black-and-red body coiled around the base of the tree.

"Don't mind him." Ratatosk strutted forward confidently. "He's all fang and no bite."

They followed behind the squirrel and approached the tree.

The serpent's head came up sharply. "Ratatosssk. How dare you bring intruders to the *sss*acred tree." Its forked tongue shot out, and yellow eyes studied each of them.

"The boss sent them." Ratatosk ran right over the snake's scaly body and up into the branches to perch. "Tell them where the chains are."

"What chain*sss*?"

"The chains to take Jormungand back to his cell."

The serpent glared at them through narrow slits. "Tho*sss*e chains belong to Odin. I'm not going to hand them over to children."

"We're not children. Calla and I are witches," Abigail said.

"And I am a son of Odin," Robert added, squaring his shoulders. "I command you to give them to us."

The serpent turned its head toward Robert. "A boy still. The dwarves of Gomorra formed those chains for Odin. He tru*sss*ts me to guard them."

"Look, there's not going to be much to guard if we don't get Jormungand locked up," Hugo argued. "Capricorn is on her way here now to destroy this place."

The snake hissed at him. "No being has the power to dessstroy this place. It is the gateway to the home of the gods."

"So you're not worried that Jormungand can slap his tail down and cause an underwater earthquake big enough to sink this whole place with you on it?" Calla asked.

The snake's tongue flicked out. "No."

"Then you're a fool," Abigail said quietly. "Vor herself came and warned me." She drew a ball of witchfire. "I won't ask again. Hand over the chains."

"I'm not afraid of witchfire," the snake hissed.

"How about now?" She threw the ball into the tree, setting one of the branches on fire.

The snake reacted in horror, swiftly snapping at the fire and swallowing it in its jaws. Smoke curled out its nostril slits as it spat the branch out on the ground. Before Abigail could move, the snake's tail shot out and wrapped her in its coils. "How dare you attack the tree of life."

"I dare because there will be no life left if we don't stop the sea serpent."

The squirrel ran up and jumped on the snake's nose, shaking its fist between the creature's eyes. "Nidhogg, enough. They speak the truth. Release her and hand over the chains."

The squirrel spoke with more authority than she expected, but it worked. The snake slowly released her and slithered back around the tree, sliding up into the branches. There was a rattle, and then something dropped to the ground at their feet. It was a silver chain no thicker than her small finger and only as long as she was tall.

"This is it?"

Ratatosk clapped his hands excitedly. "This is the chain. Take it now and go before Nidhogg changes his mind."

"But it's too small. It will never work," Abigail protested, kneeling down to finger it.

The squirrel gathered it up and tucked it into her bag, closing the flap and patting it. "Have faith, Abigail."

"We should go," Robert said. "We've been here long enough."

"Your ship is that way." The squirrel pointed into the trees. "Hurry. Time is running out."

"I don't understand how that little chain is going to stop a giant serpent," Robert said as they hurried through the trees.

"Ratatosk said we had to have faith," Calla pointed out.

"Calla's right," Hugo said. "I'll never understand how magic works. It doesn't follow scientific evidence, but I can't deny it's real. The chains must have powerful magic."

"They better," Robert grumbled. "We came a long way, only to have Odin turn his back on us."

"He didn't turn his back," Abigail said, feeling the need to defend him even though secretly she thought that was exactly what he had done. "He just . . . he's a god. He sees things differently. He must believe we can handle it."

"But why risk everything?" Robert asked. "He could have stopped the war with the witches, but he stayed out of it."

"And it turned out fine," Calla pointed out.

"Except for the fact Abigail gave the spellbook to the mermaids," he countered, then flushed. "Sorry, I didn't mean to blame you," he said to Abigail.

"It's okay. I blame myself plenty."

They arrived at the barrier of shrubs that circled the island. Robert parted them and held them open. On the other side was white sand and the sound of crashing waves.

They stepped through, only to be greeted by two bits of bad news. The first was that Jasper's ship was gone. The second was that a contingent of mermaids carrying tridents waited on the beach. Abigail recognized a redheaded one—Amarina—from her and Hugo's visit to Zequaria, the underwater city where Capricorn lived.

The mermaids pointed their tridents at them as the foursome made their way forward.

"Where is Capricorn?" Abigail demanded.

"The queen is with Jormungand, preparing to destroy this place if Odin doesn't grant an audience with her," Amarina answered, stepping forward.

"Well, start destroying it," Abigail said boldly. "Because he's not coming."

The mermaid frowned. "What do you mean?"

Abigail shrugged. "I mean he's not coming. We warned him, but he didn't seem too worried. I guess he figured we would handle it."

The mermaid looked at the others, and they all laughed. "A bunch of children?"

"Why do people keep calling us children?" Calla asked. "Abigail and I are powerful witchlings. Hugo is a Balfin and budding magic master, and Robert is a son of Odin."

The mermaids laughed again, and then Amarina's face grew taut. "If Odin doesn't show himself, then the queen will order the attack." She turned, slamming her trident into the sand.

A shockwave rumbled the ground under their feet, and then the serpent's head shot out of the water. It rose fifty feet in the air before slapping down, sending up a spray. Capricorn stood atop Jormungand's head, holding a length of seaweed that wrapped around his neck.

Abigail's heart clenched, The serpent had grown since their last encounter. It's head was even wider and its tail stretched out a mile behind him. She guided Jormungand toward the shore. Abigail and the others stepped back as his massive head slithered closer, his eyes watching them hungrily as he beached himself on the sand. Capricorn slipped down the side of his head and strode toward them.

"Abigail, we meet again," she said, sounding anything but pleased. "Tell me you have brought Odin with you."

"Sorry. He had something else to do."

"What could be more important than meeting with me?" Capricorn demanded angrily.

"He said something about taking a nap before lunch," Robert said.

Capricorn used her trident to sweep his legs out from beneath him. He landed hard on the sand, and she put one foot on his chest to hold him down. "I suggest you watch your words, or you might become Jormungand's next meal."

Next meal. That gave Abigail an idea.

"Robert here can take you to Odin." She nodded at the boy sprawled on the ground.

Capricorn kept her foot on him. "How?"

"He is a son of Odin. That's how we entered the island. Let him take you to him."

Her eyes narrowed. "Is this a trap? I demand Odin meet me here."

"Do you want to meet with him or not? We were just with him. He's not going to stick around forever."

The mermaid queen wavered.

"Or don't you want to be the goddess of the seas?" Abigail asked. "Maybe you just want to destroy everything."

"She's right," Amarina urged. "We want what is rightfully ours. The power to rule over the seas that Aegir and

Ran keep for themselves. Go see him and show him we won't be denied."

"Fine." Capricorn haughtily nodded. "You may lead me to him." She released her foot and stepped back, holding her hand out. A mermaid carrying her mother-of-pearl crown hurried forward, placed it reverently on Capricorn's head, and then bowed, moving away.

"Hugo, go with Robert," Abigail said. "We'll wait here. I have an idea," she added softly.

Hugo gave a brief nod, and the two boys walked back toward the shrub barrier. Robert parted it with both hands and held it open. The sea queen stepped through, followed by a handful of her attendants.

"What are you planning?" Amarina asked, turning to study Abigail with suspicious eyes.

"Nothing. Just waiting until they return."

The mermaid turned to speak to the other guards, and Abigail quickly leaned in to whisper in Calla's ear. "Are you ready to turn into a mermaid?"

"What do you have planned?"

"Time to bait Jormungand and see if he follows." Abigail reached out and opened Calla's bag, showing her the prickly fruit.

"Do you think he'll follow?"

"One way to find out. You'll need to swim fast—faster than that serpent. Can you do it?"

She nodded firmly and began walking toward Jormungand.

"I wouldn't get too close," Amarina said. "He has a habit of snapping up witchlings."

Calla kept walking until she was directly in front of the serpent. His eyes flickered, and his nostrils flared as she reached into her bag.

"What is she doing?" Amarina asked, tensing.

Calla held the borakora under the snout of Jormungand. She had broken it in half, and the foul stench filled the air. The serpent's eyes widened. He opened his jaws, eager to snap up Calla and the fruit, but the girl ran toward the water and nimbly dove under the waves. Abigail glimpsed a flip of her tail, and then she was zipping away from the shore. The snake jerked against the mermaid holding the seaweed leash, ripping the tether loose from her hands.

"What have you done?" Amarina screamed, but Abigail was busy giving chase, her feet pounding the sand. She flung herself at the length of seaweed dragging alongside the serpent, grabbed on with both hands, and was jerked forward into the water. Twirling from side to side, she tried to pull herself up to get air. Her head broke the surface as Jormungand chased furiously after Calla.

Water foamed around her as she held on. She pulled herself up, hand over hand, until finally she was atop the serpent. The collar of twisted seaweed around his neck had two leads to guide him. Abigail grabbed the leads and pulled back, but the serpent ignored her.

She dug Odin's chain out, trying to make sense of what to do with it. She stretched it between her hands, but it didn't change. It would never fit around Jormungand's neck. She shifted through all the hexes and spells she'd stuffed into her brain. She tried an enchanting spell that moved objects, but it just made the chain vibrate in her hands. A levitating spell lifted the chain in the air.

She could just make out Calla's flipper moving furiously through the water ahead of them. The serpent was gaining on her. It wouldn't be long before it overtook the witchling, and then what?

I can help.

Abignus.

She had been quiet for so long Abigail had hoped the dark spirit was gone.

"How?" she shouted, flinging her wet hair out of her face.

Take out the spellbook.

"I can't. I'll fall off."

Use one hand.

The bag was strapped across her body. Putting the useless chain away, she dug out the spellbook. Water dripped from the spine, but it didn't seem damaged.

"Now what?"

Open it.

Holding the book in one hand, she nudged the cover open with her chin. The wind whipped at the pages, turning them every which way until they came to a stop.

She blinked the sea spray out of her eyes. The wispy figure of Abignus rose from the pages. Wind tugged at her shadow image, blowing its hair as if the apparition were real.

They were nearly upon Calla now. Abigail saw the girl look over her shoulder as she frantically swam ahead.

"What now?" Abigail shouted as the serpent crested a wave and landed with a thump, causing her to almost drop the spellbook.

"Use the possession spell," Abignus commanded.

"I don't understand."

"I'll possess you. I can stop Jormungand. You are too weak."

Chapter 26

Hugo followed Robert back into the woods. Even though they had just come this way, everything felt different. There were no birds darting between the trees or pink fish swimming in the streams. Even the sky seemed darker, as if the world were cast in a different color. It reminded him a bit of the swamps on Balfour Island. Uninvited, an image of a viken crossed his mind. He still had nightmares about his encounter with one in the swamps.

"Do you feel it?" Robert whispered.

"Like we're somewhere else entirely?"

Robert nodded.

Fear made Hugo's pulse race and sweat trickled down his back. He studied the bushes around them, prepared to duck if anything leapt out.

"Where is Odin?" Capricorn demanded.

"He's not far." Robert stopped abruptly as the trees ended and they came out on a ledge. Before them was a massive valley of barren gray mountains spread as far as the eye could see, with no trace of vegetation.

Capricorn halted next to them with a huff. Three of her attendants joined her, looking nervous.

"What is this place?" she asked.

"I don't know. This wasn't here before." Robert looked behind them. "Didn't you have four attendants?"

Capricorn turned to study the mermaids. "Where is Livia?"

"She was just here," one of the attendants said, glancing around.

"Livia? Come out of hiding this moment," Capricorn ordered.

Behind them they heard a scream. The attendants crouched, holding their tridents before them. Then Livia came running out of the trees. "It's after me! Help!"

Capricorn stepped behind the other attendants. "What is it?"

"I don't know. I heard something and stopped to look, and. . . its eyes . . . They were horrible."

Hugo's worst fear came to life as out of the bushes appeared the hulking figure of a viken. An oversized wolf with shoulders wider than a door and fangs that glistened with drool, it prowled toward them, licking its jaws in anticipation.

"What is that?" Robert asked. He knelt down and hefted a large rock in his hand.

But Hugo was frozen with fear. He had barely escaped with his life in his last encounter. There was nothing to stop the creature from tearing them all to pieces.

"Do something," Capricorn urged, pushing her attendants forward. The mermaids looked at one another, then dropped their tridents and ran screaming back into the woods.

Robert scooped up one of the pointed weapons, holding it out in front of him. "Stay behind me, Hugo. I've got this."

Hugo's knees were knocking together so hard they were sure to be bruised. He wanted to cry, but there was no way he was going to let Robert take on the viken alone. Bending down, he reached out one shaky hand to pick up another trident.

Capricorn screeched at them, "Kill it already!"

The viken leaped at the sound of her voice, aiming its claws straight for her. As it passed between them, Hugo and Robert both plunged forward with their tridents, pinning it between them and using its momentum to fling the viken over her head and into the abyss.

It was over in an instant, but Hugo's heart wouldn't stop racing.

Robert grabbed his arm. "Are you all right? Did it scratch you?"

Hugo found his voice. "No. I'm okay. You?"

Robert grinned. "Better than that screaming ninny."

Capricorn was on the ground, her arms wrapped around her head, sounding like a cat who's tail had been stepped on. She raised her head when Robert nudged her with the trident. "Is it gone?"

"Yes. No thanks to you or your attendants."

Capricorn scrambled to her feet, smoothing down the sleek gown she wore. "I am mistress of the seas, not hairy creatures like that."

"Where did a beast like that come from?" Robert asked.

Good question, Hugo thought. "They shouldn't exist here. Melistra created the only one. I wonder though . . ."

"What?"

"Right before it appeared, I thought about vikens—and how scared I am of them."

"You think Odin conjured one up?"

Hugo shrugged. "I'm not sure. But I'm not going to think about one again."

"I've had enough of this place," Capricorn said. "Take me back to the sea this instant. If Odin thinks he can play these games with me, I will show him who has the real power when my serpent destroys this island."

Hugo and Robert kept their tridents and headed back into the woods the way they had come.

"This isn't the way," Capricorn complained as they halted at a broad river of slowly moving water. "This wasn't here before."

"There's nothing we can do but go across," Hugo said. "It doesn't look that deep." He stepped in, using the trident to steady his footing. Robert joined him, and they began making their way across.

Capricorn reluctantly followed them, grumbling loudly that she didn't like freshwater, only seawater.

As they got close to the center, the current picked up speed and the water rose, going from their knees to their waists to their chests in seconds.

"What's happening?" Hugo struggled to stay on his feet.

"I don't know," Robert said, "but I have a bad feeling."

Before they could take another step, a distant roar grew louder. Upriver, Hugo could see something moving toward them.

"What is that?" he shouted.

"It's a flood," Robert said. "Move it."

But the oncoming rush of water was flowing too swiftly. In seconds, the flood water crashed down on them, sweeping Hugo off his feet and pulling him under. The current carried him downriver. He surfaced, gasping for air, and bumped into a rock. It bruised his ribs, but he managed to hold on to the trident. Robert surfaced several feet away.

"Hugo, hang on. I'm coming." Robert swam toward him, but something stopped him.

Capricorn surfaced, grabbing on to his ankle with both hands. "Help me," she cried. "I can't swim in this awful water."

The two struggled, and Robert went under. Capricorn was panicked and latched her arms around his neck, making it impossible for the boy to swim as the current swept them all rapidly downstream.

"Let him go! You're drowning him!" Hugo shouted.

"I don't care. My life is worth more than ten of his," she cried, her face grim as she held on to the struggling boy.

Chapter 27

Hugo waited for the moment the current turned Capricorn's back to him, and then he struck, jabbing the trident into her backside. She screamed in pain and released Robert, who quickly swam away, rolling onto his back and gasping in air.

"Here." Hugo extended the trident toward a floundering Capricorn. "Hold on to the prongs, and I'll guide you."

The mermaid queen grabbed on, kicking her legs helplessly. Her red hair was plastered to her head. The water finally slowed and then grew calm. A rocky beach lined the side of the shore, and Hugo made his way toward it, towing her behind him.

Robert was there before him, kneeling and coughing up water.

Hugo's feet touched bottom. He dragged Capricorn in closer until she was able to stand.

"Why did you save her?" Robert demanded. "You should have just let her drown."

Robert was right. Without Capricorn things would be a lot easier.

"You nearly killed me!" she snarled at Hugo. "I should ram that trident down your throat."

"He saved your life," Robert said. "So if I were you, I'd be quiet."

Her hands went to her head, and she wailed. "My crown! It's come off. I can't lose it."

Hugo sighed and waded back into the river. Something sparkled in the shallows, and he dug the object out of the mud and handed it back to her. She put it firmly on her head without so much as a thank-you.

"Where are we now?" she demanded.

The barren landscape had given way to a tropical forest with lush green plants growing down to the edge of the water.

"Who knows? This place is nothing like I expected," Hugo said.

A mewling cry reached their ears.

"What is that?" Capricorn asked, her eyes wide with fear. "Another one of those beasts?"

"No. It sounds like a baby animal, or a wounded one."

He and Robert began walking toward the sound, but Capricorn jumped in their path. She wrested the trident out of Hugo's hands and pointed it at them.

"Whatever that is, it's none of our business. I need you to lead me out of here."

"We don't know where we are," Hugo said. "So we might as well see what it is."

He pushed past her, and they ducked into the thick leafy bushes. The mewling cry got closer. They emerged into a small clearing and found a baby Omera no bigger than a colt. It stood and wobbled on its taloned feet. Hugo craned his neck back. High above, just visible through the trees, was a rocky ledge.

"It must have fallen out of its nest," he said.

"Then what do we do?" Robert asked. "Can it fly?"

Hugo knelt down and reached a hand out. "Hey, little guy, are you okay?"

The baby Omera snapped at his hand, its little teeth nipping his skin. Hugo jerked his hand back. "Its wings don't look fully developed yet. He probably was able to slow his fall, but he's not strong enough to fly back up. We'll have to get him back to his mama."

"We are not going up that cliff," Capricorn said. "Leave it."

"We can't leave a baby Omera all by itself. It will starve," Hugo said. "Don't you care?"

She snorted. "I care about showing Odin I am the rightful ruler of the seas. That's what I care about."

She raised the trident over her head, prepared to throw it at the baby Omera, but Robert stepped between them. "If you throw that, you'll have to go through me."

Her nostrils flared with rage. "And what makes you think I won't?"

"Because I'm the only person who can get you out of here."

"How? You don't know where we are."

He tapped the pouch that hung around his neck. "This holds a piece of Odin's Stone. I can use it to ask Odin for help."

She slowly lowered the trident. "Then do it."

"Not until we help this baby back into its nest."

"That could take hours. How are you going to get it up that cliff?"

Robert frowned in thought. Hugo didn't know either, but they couldn't just leave it. He reached his hand out again, and this time the baby Omera let him scratch its snout.

There was a loud screech and a thumping of wings, and then a large black Omera hit the ground in a spray of dirt. It snapped at Hugo, driving him back onto his rear end.

"Stop!" Robert shouted, holding the trident in front of him. "We were only trying to help. We're friends."

The baby Omera wobbled over to Hugo and licked his face as the mother growled deep in her throat. The baby went back to its mother and spread its wings, crying and chattering away.

Robert kept the trident pointed out, but the Omera seemed to relax. Taking the baby by the nape of its neck, she chuffed out her nostrils, then sprang into the air and flew back to her nest.

"For a minute there I thought I was dinner," Hugo said and then winced as something sharp poked him in the back.

He turned slowly. Capricorn held the trident on him as she shot a triumphant look at Robert. "Show me the way out of here now or this one dies."

Robert took the pouch from around his neck and opened it, dropping the shard of Odin's Stone into his hand.

"Do you think it will work?" Hugo asked.

"It better." Robert closed his eyes, clasping the stone tightly. "Odin, please hear me. I am Robert Barconian, a descendant of your great line. Please help us get off your island. Time grows short, and we must meet our friends and stop Jormungand. Please, Odin."

The ground rumbled and shook beneath their feet. Then the earth cracked open, and they fell into a dark crevasse.

Wind whistled past Hugo's ears as they fell. His arms flailed, but there was no way to stop their descent. Capricorn screamed endlessly, her voice echoing in the vast chamber.

"What's happening?" Robert shouted.

"Tell him to stop!" Hugo shouted back.

"Odin, stop! You're going to kill us!"

They continued their headlong drop, but light appeared below them, growing larger and larger until Hugo could see sand and water.

When the ground came into view, he squinted his eyes shut as Capricorn screamed even louder. Then, with a sudden jerk, his fall was stopped, and he landed gently on the sand.

"That was amazing!" Robert jumped to his feet. "I want to go back and see Asgard all over again."

Mermaids swarmed them, pointing their tridents at the two boys while another helped Capricorn to her feet.

"Where is Jormungand?" she shouted.

Amarina looked pained. "He left, Your Highness. He is out on the seas, chasing that witchling."

"Then what are you doing here?" she screeched, stomping her foot in anger. "You should have gone in after him."

"We didn't want to leave you."

"I'll do it myself," she said, heading for the sea.

"What about them?" Amarina asked.

"Kill them." Capricorn dove into the water, followed by all the mermaids save for Amarina.

The mermaid looked uncomfortable as she held her trident. "I'm sorry. She is not herself."

"What are you going to do?" Robert asked, clenching his fists. "You can't just kill us."

"Capricorn would never forgive me if I disobeyed her." She raised the trident higher. "Just turn around so you don't have to see it."

"I'm not going to turn my back. I'm not a coward," Robert said.

"And neither am I." Hugo swallowed back the lump of fear lodged in his throat.

"Fine, have it your way."

Power crackled along the tines of the trident, and Amarina's face tightened. She was preparing to throw the weapon when a shadow appeared in the sand behind her, and another mermaid knocked the trident from her hands. The newcomer put the tines of her own trident against Amarina's throat.

Hugo recognized Calla's mother, the witch who was part mermaid.

"You would strike down children, Amarina? Is this what it's come to?"

"Calypha. You shouldn't interfere."

"Where is my daughter?"

"Probably eaten by Jormungand by now."

Amarina hissed as Calypha pressed the trident harder against her neck. "For your sake, you better hope not." She looked over at Hugo. "Do you have anything that we could use to tie her up?"

Robert took off his belt and wrapped it around the mermaid's wrists, tightening the cinch down until it was secure.

"Which way was Calla headed?" Calypha asked.

"We're not sure," Hugo said. "Abigail had some kind of plan to lure Jormungand away."

"Come, we will find them." She began walking toward the sea.

"But how will we follow? Our ship is gone."

She cupped a hand to her mouth and let out a low whinnying sound.

Two bobbing heads appeared in the water.

It was a pair of seahorses with purple-and-green scales, long narrow snouts, and bright eyes.

The boys waded out into the water. Hugo put his hands on the back of one, admiring how beautiful it was, then pulled himself onto its back. He almost fell off backward as the seahorse began moving through the water, but he grabbed the feathery tendrils along its neck and pulled himself up.

Robert was grinning from ear to ear as the seahorses carried them away from Asgard.

Hugo turned around for one last look and gasped.

The island had vanished.

Chapter 28

The wispy figure of Abignus hovered over the spell-book, while Abigail struggled to hold on to the length of seaweed and keep her balance. "You want to take control of my magic?"

"Yes. It's the only way. You're too weak," Abignus said with a sneer.

Abigail wavered. Was she weak? What did it matter who stopped Jormungand as long as he was stopped? Maybe it was easier to surrender to the darkness in her.

"Now, lest your friend be swallowed whole."

Abigail closed her eyes. She thought of Hugo and his faith in her. And Robert and his bravery. And Calla trying to outrun this giant serpent. All of them were brave no matter how bad things were. So what if she was weak? She wasn't a coward. The Norns had said dark magic wasn't bad if your heart was in the right place. She just needed to remember that.

Opening her eyes, she said, "No, I have a better idea." She slammed the spellbook shut and shoved it back in her bag, ignoring the wails of Abignus as the figure vanished into wisps of shadow.

Abigail recited the possession spell. "*Tempera similus. Tempera morpheus. Tempera transfera!*"

What are you doing! Abignus screamed, but Abigail wasn't listening.

She braced her feet, then let go of the seaweed. The familiar surge of power made her blood tingle. She started running toward the neck of the serpent, thrust her hands over her head, and dove at the creature. Her hands hit the scaly surface of his skin, but instead of bouncing off and into the ocean, she disappeared inside with a sickening slurp.

This was way different from taking possession of Hugo. Everything was black around her. It felt as if she were swimming in a pool of tar. A pressure grew in her brain, like an outside force trying to break in. She gritted her teeth and pushed back, and then she began to stretch, as if her bones had turned to liquid. Her arms and legs went numb. The serpent thrashed in the water as she struggled to gain control of his movements.

The good news was he had stopped swimming, so Calla was safe. The bad news was he was locked in a battle to expel Abigail.

His thoughts crossed hers—wordless thoughts of pent-up rage. She saw memories of him swimming in endless circles in his pen, planning his revenge. His hatred for Odin burned like a beacon. He wanted to shake the foundations of the entire world, and he didn't care what he destroyed.

Abigail put all her energy into capturing control of the beast. Power surged through her as she looked out through his eyes and saw the ocean before her.

Calla floated in the water in front of her, looking confused. The serpent shook his head from side to side, but Abigail held on to control. *This could work*, she thought.

She could control him and drive him across the sea back to his underground prison.

Suddenly the serpent went into a dive, heading straight down to the bottom. Abigail tried to pull up, but she didn't have full control. The bottom came into view. It was lined with rock and coral. He would bash himself into the ground at this rate.

Abigail forced his mouth open so that it filled with water. The snake gagged, causing him to tumble over himself so his body smashed into the seabed rather than his head. Sand swirled around, stinging his eyes. Abigail grimaced as she felt his pain, and he bellowed in rage.

She was losing her control. She tried to hold on but found herself expelled into the cold water. Terror filled her as the serpent turned. The sand settled, and his eyes glowed in the water as he swam toward her, his mouth opening to devour her.

And then someone snatched her, swooping her out of the way. Calla carried her swiftly upward and away from the serpent's jaws.

Abigail gasped in air as they surfaced.

"What happened?" Calla asked.

"I tried the possession spell, but I couldn't hold on. I was trying to give you time to get away."

I warned you! Abignus shrieked. *Now your friends will die, all because of you!*

Water frothed around them. Jormungand's head broke the surface a short distance away, and the serpent began moving toward them.

Desperation filled Abigail. She should have listened to Abignus. She was right—Abigail was too weak to defeat the serpent. She was about to beg the dark spirit to save them when a crackling line of energy shot out and wrapped around Abigail's wrists—Calla's too—and mermaids bobbed to the surface all around them. Capricorn swam in front of Jormungand and, using her fin to propel her, rose up out of the water and pointed her trident at him. Power forked out of the tines, encasing the beast's head in a net of crackling energy.

"Stop!" the mermaid queen commanded.

Jormungand howled in rage, but he flung his tail up and slowed his onslaught. Capricorn vaulted onto his head, her fin swiftly changing into legs. She grabbed hold of the seaweed ropes and knelt to rub the serpent between his eyes. "That's a good boy. Where were you running off to without me?"

The serpent grumbled in his throat, but he calmed.

Abigail struggled against her bonds, kicking her legs to stay afloat. "Capricorn, please, you must send Jormungand back. I've seen his thoughts. He's never going to stop until he's destroyed this place."

Capricorn laughed. "See how he listens to me? I am in control, not he."

"You're wrong. I was inside his head. I saw his thoughts."

"Silence!" She pointed her trident at Abigail, sending out a blast of sizzling light that turned Abigail's bones numb. "I am ruler of all living things in the seas. Watch and learn."

She put her head back and let out a high-pitched keening that reminded Abigail of the songs the whales sang as they swam past Balfour Island in the spring. Around them, sea creatures bobbed to the surface. The bulbous head of an akkar blinked at her. Several gray fins circled them in the water. She'd seen sharks swimming in the seas before, but these fins were larger than anything Abigail had encountered.

"These creatures obey my every command," Capricorn said. "You've met the akkar, but have you encountered my beautiful drekari sharks? They are the largest of their kind, specially bred to attack on my command. I'm sure they can manage a couple witchlings for breakfast."

The fins circled closer in the water.

"Or should I feed you to my pet akkar? They do get hungry."

The squid's large yellow eye blinked at them.

"What is it you want?" Abigail asked, fighting to tread water. "You already have so much power."

"But not all of it," Capricorn railed, her face mottled with rage. "I cannot make the seas rise or the waves part for me. Aegir holds the real power. Since Odin didn't see fit to see me, it appears I'll have to get his attention another way. I think I'll have Jormungand bury his little island under the sea. See how he likes that."

"Asgard is gone," a familiar voice called.

Abigail turned to find Robert and Hugo riding on the back of . . . Her jaw dropped. Were those giant seahorses?

Capricorn frowned. "What do you mean gone?"

"Asgard moves all the time," Hugo said. "It's gone."

"Then I'll find it again," she snapped.

"Doubt it," Robert said. "Not unless Odin wants you to."

"This is my sea. I know everything here."

She held the trident out. It let out a loud humming noise that rushed over the water, sending ripples. She turned slowly pointing it in a circle. After three turns she clenched her fists, screaming in frustration before gathering herself. "Fine. Maybe he'll pay attention when I destroy Garamond."

A mermaid surfaced directly in front of Abigail and Calla. "Capricorn. This has gone far enough."

Capricorn's lip drew up in a sneer. "Calypha. What are you doing here?"

"Trying to stop this insanity of yours."

"You would betray your own kind?"

"You are the one betraying all creatures of Orkney by playing this dangerous game."

Capricorn pointed her trident at Calypha. "Odin is the one who did this. I tried to be reasonable. When Garamond sinks into the sea, it is he who will be to blame." She pulled on Jormungand's leads, turning the serpent's head to the west. "Leave them to the drekari," she said to her mermaid guards before urging the serpent on.

Her band of mermaids dove underwater with a splash of their tails, following Jormungand's wake.

"Mother!" Calla threw her shackled wrists around Calypha's head. "I can't believe you're here!"

"Of course, my darling. As soon as you entered the water, I knew you were near."

"Calla, no time for reunions." Abigail eyed the circling fins that were edging closer. "I need to free my arms."

Calypha released Calla, turning to pass her hand over both their wrists. The glowing bands winked out.

"Let me deal with these pesky drekari." She put a hand to her mouth and began singing. It was a beautiful, haunting sound that sent ripples over the water. One by one the fins sank out of sight, leaving the surface calm.

Hugo urged his seahorse over and pulled Abigail up behind him.

"We have to go after her," Robert said from the back of his seahorse, his face frantic. "I have to warn my father."

They urged the seahorses on, and the sleek animals cut swiftly through the water. Calla swam alongside her mother, diving in and out of the waves.

"You okay?" Hugo asked Abigail.

"Fine. I joined with the serpent, but I wasn't strong enough."

"Then we'll have to find another way. What about Odin's chains?"

"I still don't know how to use them. They don't look like they would hold a baby shreek."

"Ratatosk said to have faith."

"Whatever that means. Can this thing go any faster?"

The seahorse was slowing. It appeared tired, its chest heaving up and down.

Calla and her mother surfaced next to them, and Robert pulled up alongside.

"Any sign of them?" he asked.

"No, they're far ahead." Calypha shook her head. "I can't feel any vibrations at all."

"I need to go faster," Abigail said. "I have to get ahead of them."

"What are you thinking?" Calla asked.

"What's the fastest animal in the sea?" Abigail asked Calypha.

"Probably the drekari. The same ones that tried to eat you earlier."

"Can you call one?"

Calypha's eyebrows went up. "Because?"

"I think I can control a shark."

"Abigail wants to possess it," Calla explained.

Calypha looked doubtful, but she put her lips together and made a humming noise, slapping at the water three times.

They waited anxiously. It didn't take long. A sleek fin broke the surface, swimming in a circle around them.

Abigail waited until it passed close by and then, muttering the words of the spell, launched off the back of the seahorse. Her hands hit the spiky rough skin, and then she disappeared inside.

Unlike the serpent, the drekari's thoughts were basic. *Hunt. Feed.*

Turning it around, she began using its powerful fins to tunnel through the water. It had endless energy. It hardly even slowed if a fish strayed too near; it simply snapped it up and kept swimming.

Abigail felt the vibrations in the water before she saw the serpent. She passed along the side of its scaly green body. Mermaids were escorting it, but none of them paid the drekari any mind. Looking upward, she could see the watery figure of Capricorn atop the serpent's head.

With a burst of speed, Abigail outpaced them.

When she surfaced, Garamond rose before her, the red flags of Skara Brae snapping in the breeze. She headed straight for the docks before ejecting herself from the shark. It immediately swam off, heading for deeper waters.

A hand reached down and hauled her up on the dock.

"Abigail? How did you get here?" Robert's father looked down at her in shock. "Do you know where Robert is?"

"Yes." She wrung out her hair. "He's on his way. So is Jormungand. He's getting bigger by the day. Soon he'll be large enough to encircle this whole island."

"What can we do?"

"He has to be returned to his underwater prison. We have chains that can bind him, but we don't know how to use them."

Water began sloshing around the dock, and the mermaid queen appeared around the edge of the bluffs skirting Skara Brae. She rode Jormungand in a circle, her trident thrust in the air. The serpent slapped its tail down, sending a shock wave under their feet. The dock swayed, nearly knocking them off. The cliffside rumbled, as rocks fell into the sea, and then the wall of the stone fortress cracked in a zigzag line up the side.

"She's trying to bring the walls down!" Lord Barconian shouted.

Abigail created a large ball of witchfire and threw it directly at Capricorn. It sailed across the water, but the mermaid queen batted it away with her trident, turning to look furiously at Abigail.

"Capricorn, please listen!" Abigail shouted. "You must stop this."

She urged Jormungand closer to shore. "Odin continues to ignore me, so I will destroy everything he professes to love."

"That's not what a goddess would do," Abigail said. "The gods are here to protect us and guide us, not take what isn't theirs."

She scrunched her nose with disdain. "What do you know of the gods?"

"I know that they are not perfect, but they are wiser than we know."

She thrust the trident at the sky. "If Odin is so wise, then where is he? Why does he not stop me from destroying his precious islands?"

Abigail wondered the same thing but she kept her head high. "Because he trusts me to stop you."

The mermaid queen tilted her head back, howling with laughter. "Watch and learn witchling. And see the true power of my serpent."

She turned Jormungand and headed back out to sea.

"What is she doing?" Lord Barconian asked.

"I don't know."

Waves began to rise, swelling and crashing against the dock. The ships creaked and thrashed on their moorings.

"Get back!" Lord Barconian shouted.

They cleared the docks and moved higher on the shore, the same shore Abigail had stood on a few short months ago, feeling victorious after defeating Vertulious.

Suddenly the water receded, leaving bare wet sand and a few flopping fish. The water rolled back farther and farther.

"Everyone, leave the shore now!" Lord Barconian shouted. "She's creating a tidal wave!"

Chapter 29

The frightened Orkadian soldiers threw down their weapons and ran up the hill. Lord Barconian tried to usher her away, but Abigail shrugged free.

"No. I have to fix this."

A giant wall of water began to form, rolling over and over on itself as more water receded. It spread in either direction as far as the eye could see, rising as high as the walls of the fortress.

"If that wave continues to grow, it will wipe out everything it touches," Robert's father warned. "We must go."

Ignoring his pleas, Abigail walked out into the wet sand, trying to focus. Her mind was blank. It was too big. Too much water. Nothing in her powers would be able to stop it. So this was it. The end. She was almost relieved. The water would wash her away, and that would be that.

It's time. Let me help you.

Abigail started, so focused on the problem at hand she had almost forgotten about her darker half. "How?"

The spellbook. Open it.

Abigail reached into the book bag still strapped across her chest and pulled out the sodden book. She opened the cover, and Abignus trickled up in a wispy image, looking triumphant.

"That's better." Abignus turned and studied the wall of water. "I can stop it."

"How? Show me and I'll do it."

"Now where's the fun in that?" she said with a pout. "Trade places with me, and I'll handle it."

"No."

"Then it was nice knowing you." She waggled her fingers goodbye and started to disappear back into the book.

"Wait!"

The wispy figure paused.

"How do we change places?"

"You just say the possession spell and dive into the spellbook."

"And then how do we change back?"

"Just push me out when you don't need me."

Abigail hesitated. "I don't trust you."

Abignus laughed. "I know. But really, I am you, so you don't trust yourself."

Abigail's heart pounded in her chest. The wave had grown even higher. White foam coursed over the top. Any moment now it was going to be unleashed on this island, and countless lives would be lost.

"Fine." She recited the spell quickly before she could change her mind. As the last word passed her lips, the wispy figure of Abignus flew straight into her mouth.

Abigail dropped the spellbook as a fizzy feeling entered her bloodstream, and then cold spread through her veins like liquid ice, weighing her down and leaving her sluggish and dizzy. Pressure grew inside her head, pushing her control aside.

It was as if a string had been cut, and Abigail was no longer in charge. She could see through her eyes and feel the wind on her face, but she was an observer in her own body. She tried to raise her hands, but they wouldn't move.

"Now this is nice," she said, only it wasn't her speaking. This dark presence had taken over her mind, sitting there like a cold reptile, unblinking and unfeeling.

Stop the wave, Abigail urged.

"Patience, blue witch. I'm in charge now."

So now she was the blue witch. Abigail was helpless as her feet danced along the sand, her hands splayed out, laughing as though she hadn't a care in the world.

If that wave crashes on us, we'll die the same as everyone else, Abigail reminded her.

Her dark half sighed and opened the spellbook. "You're no fun at all. Let's see, what was I planning? Oh, here it is."

She snapped the book shut, shoving it back in the book bag, and cocked her head to the side.

"Time to fire up some magic." Abignus ran her hands in a circle, calling up a strange ball of yellow witchfire that crackled with a powerful energy Abigail had never felt before. Her dark witch had pried open a new well of power, unleashing a magic she hadn't known was there. "Yes, you've been hiding this, haven't you?"

Abigail was helpless to do anything but watch as the dark witch spread her arms out.

"It's a simple protection spell any firstling can do. Just with a little kick."

Energy crackled in the air as the strange ball of yellow witchfire grew larger, and then Abignus thrust her hands forward, shouting, "*Escudo maligna.*"

Escudo was a spell Abigail had used many times. It

cast a protective shield around the wielder. But how was casting a shield going to stop this monstrous wave?

With her hands extended, Abignus stomped her foot into the ground. The yellow ball of witchfire flew forward, spreading out into a glowing wall. Magic continued to pour from her hands, and the wall grew higher and higher until it matched the height of the wave.

"You can help, you know," Abignus said. "Quit fighting me."

Abigail hesitated, fearing what would happen if she let down the thin barrier that protected her from this other dark presence. As if she could be swept away and erased from existence if she wasn't careful.

"Now, blue witch," Abignus said with a grunt. The effort was clearly taxing her.

Abigail relaxed the hold she'd placed on her mind and let herself join with this new power flowing through her. At once, the protective wall jumped higher and shot along the length of the sand, wrapping the coast in a shimmering barrier. The giant wave was visible through it.

Will it hold? she asked.

"If you don't distract me."

The wave crested, rolling forward at an impossible speed as it raced toward the shore and the innocent people in the fortress. It crashed against the shield like a thousand battering rams hitting at once. The jolt nearly knocked the dark witch off her feet.

"Give me everything," Abignus demanded. "You're still holding back."

Abigail had no choice but to release every last grip she had on herself. She lowered her defenses completely, and with a crack she felt in her spine, the last bit of her reserve washed away in the tide of power surging into her hands.

But the shield held.

The water receded, finding no way forward. Abigail silently cheered—until suddenly the giant head of the serpent burst out of the water, soaring into the sky and crashing down on the barrier.

Their hold on the spell shattered. Water rushed forward.

Run, Abigail urged.

Abignus raced toward higher ground as water rushed toward them. The wall had done the job of stopping the worst of it, but there was still a large swell bearing down on them.

Abignus turned her head. Capricorn rode atop Jormungand. She thrust her trident forward and shot a bolt of lightning at their feet, sending them tumbling over and over on the sand. Water washed over them, rolling them under, but the dark witch kicked off the bottom and drove them to the surface. They were swept against the piling of the dock. Abignus grabbed on with both hands as the receding water tried to suck them out to sea, and then it was over.

Abignus swam the short distance to shore, and hands reached down and helped them onto the sand.

"Are you all right?" Lord Barconian asked. He was surrounded by a small band of soldiers. The entire shore had been wiped out. Several of the warships were submerged, their masts broken in half.

But the fortress still stood.

"I'm fine," the dark witch said, shaking free of his grasp.

Abigail could make out Robert and Hugo on the backs of their seahorses, with Calla and her mom swimming next to them.

Capricorn urged Jormungand closer to shore, her eyes blazing with rage. "This isn't finished." She raised the trident over her head, about to throw it directly at Abigail, when a bolt of lightning cut the sky.

"Capricorn. That is enough," Odin said in a thunderous voice. The mighty god stood on the shore, hands on his hips.

The mermaid queen's eyes lit up as she pulled Jormungand up at the edge of the sand. "Odin, at last you've seen reason."

"No. I see a spoiled, selfish woman who has let her love of power get the best of her."

She gasped at his insult. "It is you who are selfish with your gifts of power. I deserve to be ruler of the seas, not Aegir."

"No, you failed every test I gave you."

Her face contorted with shock. "What tests?"

"When you were on my island. I was willing to entertain the idea of giving you what you wanted, but you failed."

"How? That's not fair!" she protested. "I didn't know you were testing me."

"To be a god, you must set aside what is best for yourself and think of the people you rule over, the ones who look to you for guidance."

"I would never harm a creature in the sea," she said.

"And yet, you let your own attendants risk their lives with that viken while you cowered behind them."

She sniffed, dismissing him with a wave of her hand. "They live to serve me."

"No, the gods live to serve others. The boy is a descendant of mine, and you would have let him drown in the river to save yourself."

"My life is more valuable than his!" she protested.

"No life is more valuable than another. That baby Omera was helpless, yet you would have let it perish."

She shrugged. "That creature is not under my command."

"All creatures are under our command. And this is why you have failed my tests. Due to your reckless behavior, you will be stripped of your title and forbidden from entering the seas ever again. I release the mermaids under your command to return to their home with Aegir or stay in Zequaria. It is their choice."

Rage colored her cheeks bright red. "How dare you! I am queen of the mermaids. You cannot take that away."

"Watch me."

Odin flicked his wrist, and her crown of pearl went spinning off in the air. As Capricorn reached for it, she lost her grip on Jormungand's reins and teetered off into the water. She began to flounder, splashing about, then slipped under the surface with a strangled gasp.

Hugo and Robert rode up on their seahorses and each took an arm, dragging her toward the shore until they were close enough to jump in the water and help her onto dry sand. Calla and her mother emerged, their mermaid tails quickly separating into legs.

Calypha carried the pearl crown in her hands.

"It is yours if you want it," Odin said. "The mermaids need someone to lead them."

She hesitated, but Calla elbowed her. "Do it, Mother. You will be a great queen."

Calypha slowly put the crown on her head. Capricorn's trident flew into her hands.

"Give me back my powers!" Capricorn screamed, slamming her fists into the sand.

"I rather think we've heard enough out of you." Odin snapped his fingers, and her lips sealed so that she couldn't speak.

A pair of Orkadian soldiers hauled her up and dragged her away.

The serpent wasn't moving; he just eyed them with his reptilian eyes, as if waiting for something.

Odin turned and patted Abigail on the shoulder. "It looks like you've done a fine job."

"Thanks."

We're done here. Let me back, Abigail said.

Not likely. I'm not finished.

And then Abigail realized what the dark witch intended. When she had merged with Jormungand, she wasn't the only one who had forged a connection with that horrid serpent.

She opened her mouth to warn Odin, but nothing came out.

Abigail felt a surge of power as her hand twitched at her side, unseen by the others. A strange electric current appeared around Odin's feet. He looked down, puzzled. A pair of glowing rings encircled his ankles. He tried to lift his leg, but he couldn't move.

"What is this? Who is playing a trick on me?"

And then Jormungand struck, lunging out of the sea and launching himself at the god. Odin hardly had time to raise his arms up to protect himself as the serpent's jaws closed in.

Abigail used every ounce of mental strength to free herself. She managed to get one leg to obey her, using it to kick Odin to the side so that the serpent's jaws snapped closed on air.

The god hissed and grabbed his arm. The serpent's tooth had grazed him, leaving a red welt. He struck back, sending a bolt of lightning that caused the serpent's whole body to be encased in a glowing halo, paralyzing him within a powerful field of energy.

"Don't just stand there, Abigail. Give him the chains." Hugo reached into the book bag and pulled them out before Abignus could stop him. "How do we use these?" he asked Odin.

"Where did you get these? Ah, Ratatosk, bless that squirrel." He lifted the chains over his head and threw them in a lasso that stretched into a larger and larger loop. They glowed with a white fire. The loop dropped around the neck of the serpent, and he tightened the noose.

"Time to take you back where you belong," Odin said, and then he stumbled, dropping to his knees.

Abigail felt the triumph in the dark witch rise up.

"The serpent's bite has a poison," Odin gasped out. "One powerful enough . . . to bring down . . . even a god such as I." He sank back on the sand, his face pale.

Abigail stood helpless. Was this going to be another disaster that was all her fault?

"Wait!" Hugo dropped onto his knees next to Odin. He reached into his bag and pulled out an apple, polishing it on his sleeve. "Maybe this will help."

Odin coughed weakly. "Only an apple of the gods can save me, boy."

"Trust me." He put it to Odin's mouth.

Odin took a bite, then another. Color returned to his cheeks. He ate the entire thing down to the core, and slowly the mark on his arm faded. He breathed a deep sigh of relief. "That's better." Robert helped him up. Odin looked sternly at Hugo. "Should I ask where you got an apple of the gods?"

Hugo grinned. "Probably not."

Odin shook his head. "It is not often I am surprised, but today has been full of them. It is time I return home." He patted Abigail on the head, a slight frown on his brows. "You saved me, witchling. If that serpent had bit me fully, a single apple would not have saved me. I am in your debt. I must return to Asgard. Calypha, can I trust you to show them the way to Aegir's home?"

The new mermaid queen nodded her head, and in a swift bolt of lightning, Odin was gone.

Abigail grinned inside. Hugo had saved Odin! He must have found the apple tree Vertulious had planted, although why he had kept it a secret from her, she had no idea.

Calla stood next to her. "Time to take Jormungand home. Abigail and I will lead him. Hugo, Robert, you take the seahorses."

"Can I, Father?" Robert asked.

His father sighed. "When have I ever been able to stop you having an adventure?"

Robert grinned, and then a look of horror crossed his face, and his hand went to his satchel. "Oh no. Father . . . I lost it."

"Lost what?"

"Your compass. I borrowed it to find Asgard. I left it on Jasper's ship, but the ship was gone when we returned to the beach. How can you ever forgive me?"

His father looked grave, but he just squeezed Robert's shoulder. "You are worth far more to me than an old compass. We will have to hope it turns up one day."

Abigail could sense her dark witch struggling, wanting to somehow change the outcome. In the end, Abignus gave in and followed Calla, climbing up the length of seaweed on top of Jormungand. The serpent was furious, but the magic in the chains kept him subdued.

Grasping the chain, Calla guided him away from the shore and out into the water. Calypha swam ahead, leading the way. Mermaids surrounded her on all sides. They had taken the change in leadership well.

Calla turned to look at her. "You seem awfully quiet."

"I'm fine," Abignus bit out.

Calla studied her, then looked away. "It's okay if you used dark magic. It doesn't make you anything you don't want to be."

Abigail wanted to laugh at that. Calla didn't know how wrong she was.

They moved swiftly across the water. Abigail tried everything she could think of to try to communicate with Calla and let her know what was happening, but Abignus kept firm control over her.

In front of them, Calypha held her hand up. The water swirled, and then a giant eddy appeared, growing wider and wider. Riding up and out of it was a man astride a seahorse larger than theirs. He wore a crown and carried a golden trident.

Aegir.

"I see you've brought my guest home," he said, eyeing Calypha's crown curiously. "We haven't met."

She rose out of the water, using her powerful tail, and bowed her head. "I am Calypha, the new queen of the mermaids. I hope we can work together to watch over the seas."

"I'd like nothing better, although I would appreciate it if you would see to the release of my son Jasper. I believe he is in one of your cells."

"It will be my first action as queen," she said.

He motioned to the mermen in the water to take the chains. "We can take it from here."

Calla dove into the water. Abignus slid down the side of Jormungand onto the back of Hugo's seahorse.

Robert rode up next to them, grinning. "Well, that was an adventure. I can't wait to have another."

"I think I can wait a year or two," Hugo said, grinning back.

Robert looked at Abigail. "You saved Garamond. I will be forever indebted to you, witchling."

Abigail wanted to shout at him that he wasn't speaking to Abigail, but he just winked and rode off, waving goodbye.

Calla bobbed in the water next to them. "Race you home," she said, flashing a smile.

"No fair!" Hugo said as she disappeared with a flash of her tail. He urged the seahorse after her.

Abigail felt her arms clench around Hugo's waist.

It would be so easy to knock him into the open seas, Abignus said. *He wouldn't last long out here.*

No! That's enough. I want you gone now!

She could hear Abignus chuckle.

That's never going to happen. From now on, I run the show.

Abigail tried desperately to think of a way to eject her dark shadow. Jormungand had done it by threatening to impale himself on the ground. Maybe if she tried that.

I can read your thoughts, you know, and that won't work. You can't hurt me without hurting yourself.

Abigail fumed, feeling helpless as they sped across the water. Hugo chattered on as if he hadn't a care in the world.

Chapter 30

Something was terribly wrong, although Hugo was doing everything in his power to act normal. Abigail wasn't herself. He had seen something on the beach—right before Odin was struck—as if Abigail were fighting with herself. Her hands had twitched, and her eyes had flickered from bright green to a dark shade he had seen on more than one occasion.

The island of Balfour came into sight. Hugo slowed the seahorse down until they were close to shore, then jumped in knee-deep water and helped Abigail down.

Calla floated next to her mother. "Go ahead. I'll be along as soon as I say goodbye."

Abigail turned her back, trudging along the path and ignoring Hugo like he wasn't there.

"Abigail." He put his hand on her arm.

She stopped. Her body was trembling, as if she were cold or frightened.

"Is everything okay? You seem different."

"I'm fine," she said woodenly. "Just tired."

"We really fixed things this time, didn't we? Everything is back as it should be."

Abigail trembled harder, her whole body shaking, and then she slowly turned around to face Hugo. He gasped. He hardly recognized her. Her eyes had gone completely dark, almost black, and her chin was down so she was glaring up at him.

"You're a fool, Hugo Suppermill. I don't know why I ever wasted time on you." Her voice dripped with contempt.

"Abigail, please stop. You're not yourself."

She laughed harshly. "I have never been more myself. This is who I am, Hugo. And I think the world has had enough of you." A glowing ball of witchfire appeared in her hand, and she cocked it back. "Say goodbye."

He wanted to run, but there was something so odd about the whole scene—almost as if someone had taken over the Abigail he knew. A sudden thought struck him.

"You're not the real Abigail, are you? Whoever you are, you used the possession spell on her. Abigail, if you're in there, you can fight this."

The Abigail in front of him laughed. "Fool, she traded places with her dark witch, and now she will never be set free. We will be one, and our power will be unstoppable. The only thing holding us back is weak friends like you."

She drew her arm back, ready to send the blazing witch-fire at him. And then she jerked as the ball of witchfire flew out of her hand, landing harmlessly over Hugo's head.

"Run, Hugo!"

Abigail was contorting, her body spasming and jerking out of control. Her face shifted several times from calm to angry, her eyes changing color back and forth from green to black.

THE MERMAID QUEEN

Hugo didn't know what to do. He wanted to run and get Calla, but he didn't dare leave Abigail. He had to get that dark witch out of her.

Taking his medallion from around his neck, he held it in front of him and said the words. "*Tempera similus. Tempera morpheus. Tempera transfera.*"

He didn't know if it would drive the dark presence from her, but he dove at her.

It didn't work as he expected. His magic wasn't strong enough for him to merge with Abigail, but the force of his impact shattered the other one's hold on her. Suddenly there were two Abigails standing there, one shadowy and one solid.

The real Abigail moved to his side. "Hugo, you did it!"

The shadowy figure circled them. "Why do you fight me? We are on the same side."

"I will never be on your side," Abigail said. "You are nothing but evil."

"Witches are meant to be evil. What is it about this boy that makes you so weak?"

"He is my friend."

"Witches do not have friends."

"This one does."

The wispy image mocked her. "Then that is why you will fail, Abigail Tarkana. You are not worthy of being a witch."

"Maybe it's time for the witches to change," Abigail countered. "To become something more."

Abignus laughed. "You are right about that. It is time for a change. Too bad you won't be part of it."

The dark witch's face warped as it shot toward Abigail. Hugo tackled his friend to the ground, and it sailed past their heads, disappearing into the woods.

"Is it gone?" Abigail asked.

"I think so." He helped her to her feet. "What was that?"

"Me," she said simply.

"What do you mean?"

"Abignus was my dark magic come to life."

He frowned. "But how is that possible?"

"The spellbook," Abigail said bitterly. "Every time I called on it, it's like I left a part of myself there. Abignus knew everything about me, parts of my magic I didn't even know were there. Face it, Hugo, she is me."

"Then why did you try to stop her?" he demanded. "Why did you try to save me? Save Odin? Why didn't you just let her have her way?"

She stared at him, and he watched as waves of pain washed over her. "I don't know. But whatever I did, it wasn't enough, was it? That thing is still out there." She fumbled in her bag and yanked the spellbook out. "Maybe it's time I got rid of this once and for all. Can you gather some wood?"

He piled up handfuls of twigs and dead limbs, then Abigail sparked it with witchfire. She opened the cover. "Vertulious, if you're in there, come out."

The pages were quiet, and then there was a faint whisper of air, and a haggard-looking Vertulious trickled into view.

"What have you done?" he asked, his voice a raspy whisper.

"I've finally fixed everything," she said. "And I'm ready to set you free, but first, you said the spellbook had a new master. Tell me who it is."

But his eyes were frightened. "Something is wrong. The magic is gone."

"What do you mean?"

"Look for yourself. The pages of the spellbook are empty."

Abigail flipped through the book. "Hugo, he's right. All the pages are blank. Who did this?"

Vertulious rubbed at his temples. "It was a powerful witch. Capricorn took the spellbook to her before giving it to you. The witch did something to it. I felt the jolt of magic. Whatever you started, this isn't finished."

"But who was it? Please, I need to know."

"I didn't see her face, only felt her powers. But she had something of yours."

"What?"

"A trace of your blood she made into a powerful potion and then sprinkled on the pages. I felt it when you used the healing spell. A drop of your blood fell onto the page, and the spellbook recognized it. Like it was the key to unlocking a very dark spell."

Abigail went silent. "But who has that kind of power? Hestera?"

Vertulious shook his head. "I'm sorry, witchling. I can be of no further use. If you please, I'd like to see what comes next."

He bowed his head and disappeared back into the spellbook.

Abigail closed the book and then tossed it into the fire. It burned bright green for a moment, and then the flames returned to orange. The pages curled into ash until all that was left were a few pieces of charred spine. She toed them with her boot, making sure every last piece was gone.

"Who do you think is behind this?" Hugo asked.

"I don't know. And how did they get some of my blood?"

Hugo snapped his fingers. "The wraiths. They took the shard of ice."

Abigail's face paled. "You think this witch can control the wraiths?"

"If she can, then she has very dark powers indeed," Hugo said. "I wonder though . . ."

"What?"

"It's just . . . Abignus was nothing like you."

She bit her lip, looking unconvinced. "Why do you say that?"

"Abigail, that thing was evil and cold. It had no heart. You have a heart, a big one."

She laughed, though it was wobbly. "I'm a witch, Hugo. Our hearts are made of stone."

"Maybe some of them but not yours. I swear on all I know, that's the truth."

"Then how about this for truth. I hated Abignus, but now I almost miss her. She tapped into powers I didn't know I had. Without her, I feel like less of a witch. As horrible as she was, she was me, Hugo, so it's like part of me is missing now."

Hugo thought back on his days of marching with the Balfin Boys' Brigade. "You think I didn't like parts of being a soldier?"

She scoffed. "You hated every bit of it."

"Mostly, but there were times I liked it. I felt stronger, and my parents were proud of me for the first time. It was easier than having to think all the time. Listen, Abigail, what if Abignus wasn't you? What if whoever is behind this made her up?"

Abigail went still. "But she knew everything about me."

He shrugged. "That doesn't prove anything."

Disappointment clouded her face. "It also doesn't prove you're right. But thank you, Hugo, for always believing in me. I don't know what I would do without you."

He gripped her shoulder. "I'm not going anywhere. We'll find out who's behind this, I promise. And hey, at least the world isn't in mortal danger this time."

That got her to smile. "True. I just have to pass all my exams so I can continue being a witch, and then we'll get to the bottom of who Capricorn was working with. I have a feeling it's bad news for the coven."

Chapter 31

After determining the rickety sailboat had a better chance of getting off Asgard than her rowboat, Endera had done her best to guide it home. It had flown surprisingly quick over the waters, as if the wind favored its sails. It seemed to have a mind of its own when it came to steering, so she had given up and let it have its way.

Relief left her weak-kneed when she spied the familiar outline of Balfour Island at dusk. *Home.* She had thought she might never see it again. Guiding the ship to an open slip, she stepped onto the dock, sinking to her knees in relief. Damarius brushed up against her, panting his excitement at being home. She rubbed his head, silently thanking him for his company, then watched as the wolf bounded into the woods, as eager as she to be on dry land.

She still hadn't made her mind up how to proceed. Odin was their sworn enemy, but Madame Hestera had wanted to warn him, or had she? Who was behind his attempted poisoning and why? Who could she trust? In the end, she decided to head straight for Madame Hestera's chambers and tell her everything that had happened. She would hope for the best and adjust her story depending on how the leader of the coven reacted.

She knocked on the heavy wooden door and waited. After a moment, a chair scraped, and the doorknob twisted. Madame Hestera peered out, eyeing the hall, then yanked her inside.

"What do you want, child?" Her eyes looked frightened and her hair was astray.

"I'm sorry, Madame Hestera, I shouldn't have bothered you." Endera turned, wanting to hurry away, but the old witch grabbed her shoulder with clawlike fingers and spun her around.

"Tell me what you came to say and hold nothing back."

"I stole the message for Odin and delivered it to him myself, only it was poisoned, which you probably already know. He didn't touch it. He knew somehow."

"Poisoned." Madame Hestera paled, and her hand loosened. She moved away, sinking down in her chair by the fire. "What did he do?"

"He told me to come back here and say thank you. That he believed me and . . ." Endera hesitated.

"What?" Madame Hestera's eyes swiveled to pierce the witchling where she stood.

"That we have a bigger problem in our coven. That someone has betrayed us."

Hestera seemed to age in front of Endera. She closed her eyes as if she were thinking. When they opened, they had regained some of their fierceness. "Tell no one of this. Do you hear me?"

Endera nodded.

"What of the map?" She held her hand out.

Endera looked down in shame. "The map was lost. But I found this." She pulled out the heavy brass compass from her bag and held it out. "I think they used it to find Asgard."

Hestera took it and nodded. "It will come in handy. If you value your position in this coven, your lips will remain sealed. There is a vermin among us, someone who has burrowed themselves in deep. It will not be easy to root them out. I have an idea who's behind this, but it will take the utmost secrecy to foil her. I will need your help. There are few I can trust."

"You can trust me," Endera said, drawing herself up taller. "I will do anything for this coven."

Epilogue

Calla left her mother, wiping away a tear. It was always sad when she said goodbye, but her mother was determined to help the mermaids after Capricorn's fall from grace.

As she made her way back to the Tarkana Fortress, a whisper of noise in the brush tickled her ears, but she paid it no heed. The whisper grew louder until it penetrated her thoughts.

If you had more power, you could bring your mother home forever.

Calla smiled. "I don't need her home forever," she said, then wondered why she had spoken aloud.

But you want power, the voice whispered.

"Of course." Calla spoke aloud again. "Every witch does. Who are you?" She stopped and turned around in the clearing to see who was speaking in her ear, but there was no one, just shadows dancing on the edges.

I am an ally who can get you what you want.

Calla blinked. "And what do I want?"

Power. Enough power to rule the coven.

"My great-aunt Hestera rules the coven." Calla bit her lip. "I would never betray her."

But you would betray your friends to get what you want?

Stung, Calla retorted, "No, I would not."

But you did once.

"When?" *This was an odd conversation*, she thought.

When you were a glitch-witch and wanted your magic. Remember? You were willing to do whatever it took to get it, even steal the spellbook from your friend. Abigail was nearly expelled.

An ugly feeling arose in Calla, an urge that had long been there—to take what she wanted no matter the cost. She squashed it down before it could take hold. "True. But it wasn't very nice. Besides, I didn't have a choice."

So your magic is more important than your friends?

"I suppose . . . What does it matter? Without my magic, they wouldn't even bother with me."

And what of dark magic? You like using it.

Calla shuddered. "No. Not really."

You said you quite liked how it felt when you lifted the ship out of the water.

Calla's heart tripped in her chest. "I admit I liked it, but I was frightened of it."

You can learn to wield it with confidence. If you had to choose between your coven and your friends, what would you choose?

"My coven, of course."

Then you are the one.

Calla gasped as a figure materialized in front of her. It was the High Witch, Anarae. At her side was a shadowy figure about the same size as Calla. The features were wispy but she thought it looked a bit like Abigail.

"I think you will make the perfect apprentice." Anarae

snapped her fingers, and the shadowy figure shot forward and disappeared inside Calla.

Calla's face slowly changed, her features sharpening, her eyes darkening. She looked wonderingly down at her hands, flexing them as if for the first time.

Anarae smiled. "Welcome back, Abignus."

THE END

From the Author

*D*ear Reader:

I hope you enjoyed *The Mermaid Queen*! It continues to be so much fun delving into the past of my favorite *Legends of Orkney*™ characters. I love finding out more about Sam Baron's mom, Abigail, and how she got her start at the Tarkana Witch Academy.

As an author, I love to get feedback from my fans letting me know what you liked about the book, what you loved about the book, and even what you didn't like. You can write me at PO Box 1475, Orange, CA 92856, or e-mail me at author@alaneadams.com. Visit me on the web at www.alaneadams.com and learn about starting a book club with my *Witches of Orkney*, *Legends of Olympus*, or *Legends of Orkney*™ series, or invite me to visit your school to talk about reading!

I want to thank my son Alex for inspiring me to write these stories, and his faith in me that I would see them through. To my wonderful twitter teachers who share my stories with their students—thank you for encouraging a new generation of readers! To my amazing foundation director, Lauri, a million thanks for your willingness to do read-alouds with me again and again. And of course a big shoutout to the team at SparkPress for their unfailing support. Go Sparkies!

Look for more adventures with Abigail and Hugo as they face a perilous future in *The Dark Witch*, coming Fall 2022.

To Orkney! Long may her legends grow!

—Alane Adams

About the Author

Alane Adams is an author, professor, and literacy advocate. She is the author of the Legends of Orkney™ and Legends of Olympus and Witches of Orkney fantasy mythology series for tweens and *The Coal Thief, The Egg Thief, The Santa Thief,* and *The Circus Thief* picture books for early-grade readers. She lives in Southern California.

Author photo © Steve Lopushinsky/Turville Photography

SELECTED TITLES FROM SPARKPRESS

SparkPress is an independent boutique publisher delivering high-quality, entertaining, and engaging content that enhances readers' lives, with a special focus on female-driven work. www.gosparkpress.com

Eye of Zeus: Legends of Olympus Book 1, Alane Adams. $12.95, 978-1-68463-028-8. Finding out she's the daughter of Zeus is not what a foster kid like Phoebe Katz expected to hear from a talking statue of Athena. But when her beloved social worker is kidnapped, Phoebe and her two friends must travel back to ancient Greece and rescue him before she accidentally destroys Olympus.

The Blue Witch: The Witches of Orkney, Book 1, Alane Adams. $12.95, 978-1-943006-77-9. Nine-year-old Abigail Tarkana has a problem: her witch magic has finally come in, but it's *different*—and being different is a problem at the Tarkana Witch Academy. Together with her scientist-friend Hugo, she face off against sneevils, shreeks, and vikens in a race to discover the secrets about her mysterious magic.

Red Sun: The Legends of Orkney, Book 1, Alane Adams. $17, 978-1-940716-24-4. After learning that his mom is a witch and his missing father is a true Son of Odin, 12-year-old Sam Baron must travel through a stonefire to the magical realm of Orkney on a quest to find his missing friends and stop an ancient curse.

Wendy Darling: Volume 1, Stars, Colleen Oakes. $17, 978-1-94071-6-96-4. Loved by two men—a steady and handsome bookseller's son from London, and Peter Pan, a dashing and dangerous charmer—Wendy realizes that Neverland, like her heart, is a wild place, teeming with dark secrets and dangerous obsessions.

The Thorn Queen:A Novel, Elise Holland. $16.95, 978-1-943006-79-3. Twelve-year-old Meylyne longs to impress her brilliant, sorceress mother—but when she accidentally breaks one of Glendoch's First Rules, she accomplishes the opposite of that. Forced to flee, the only way she may return home is with a cure for Glendoch's diseased prince.

Above the Star: The 8th Island Trilogy, Book 1, Alexis Chute. $16.95, 978-1-943006-56-4. *Above the Star* is an epic fantasy adventure experienced through the eyes of three unlikely heroes transported to a new world: senior citizen Archie; his daughter-in-law, Tessa; and his fourteen-year-old granddaughter, Ella. In this otherworldly realm, all interests are at war, all love is unrequited, and everyone is left to unravel the truth of who they really are.

About SparkPress

SparkPress is an independent, hybrid imprint focused on merging the best of the traditional publishing model with new and innovative strategies. We deliver high-quality, entertaining, and engaging content that enhances readers' lives. We are proud to bring to market a list of *New York Times* best-selling, award-winning, and debut authors who represent a wide array of genres, as well as our established, industry-wide reputation for creative, results-driven success in working with authors. SparkPress, a BookSparks imprint, is a division of SparkPoint Studio LLC.

Learn more at GoSparkPress.com